TRAPPED

TED BAGLEY

Life isn't tied with a bow, but it's still a gift.

—Regina Brett, age ninety

I refuse to accept the idea that man is mere flotsam and jetsam in the river of life unable to influence the unfolding events which surround him. I refuse to accept the view that mankind is so tragically bound to the starless midnight of racism and war that the bright daybreak of peace and brotherhood can never be a reality.

I refuse to accept the cynical notion that nation after nation must spiral down a militaristic stairway into the hell of thermonuclear destruction. I believe that unarmed truth and unconditional love will have the final word in reality. This is why right . . . temporarily defeated . . . . is stronger than evil triumphant.

—Dr. Martin Luther King Jr.

CONTENTS

ACKNOWLEDGMENTS

Darkness can be a condition of time or a state of mind. No matter the choice, it represents a period of uncertainty, possible confusion, and hopelessness. As a result of the darkness dilemma, I have decided to put on paper my feelings about this dilemma from a common perspective. As kids, most of us were afraid of the dark primarily because of the stories that our parents and grandparents would tell us about the supernatural and other creepy things that only come out in darkness. Naturally, we believed it because it came from people close to us who were very credible in our eyes no matter what stories were put before us. In a way, it was good because in the early stage of development, it's important that we develop our imagination which would eventually play a major role in our ability to focus on what could be versus what is.

The title of this work is *Trapped* . Now you may ask, what's so significant about this subject? Feeling Trapped and in the dark can be a frightening thing, especially if it's not by choice. Things are so much clearer when there is defining light. Try walking into a room that is pitch-dark, even if it's in your own home, and you will see how difficult it is to navigate around objects that you are familiar with and pass every day while there is light. Most tragedies generally happen under the cover of darkness. If being in the dark is not where you want to be, then what are you doing about it? The real answer is to turn the light on. If only it were that easy. Think of how you feel when you are sitting in a small room with no windows and sometimes only one way out. You can feel trapped.

Mama would say, "Boy, turn on the light in that room. Can't you see how dark it is?" Mama was afraid that I would stumble over something and break some of her valuable whatnots. A whatnot was considered any little glass or porcelain figure used to decorate book cases, dressers, and nightstands. See, if you read my books, you will pick up a lot of terms and information that you didn't know or, for those baby boomers, hadn't thought about for many years.

What Mama didn't realize at the time was that she was stating a condition that would exist for many generations of men of color. Somewhere in the growing-up process, we got off track, lost our way to the light switch, and found that we were in pitch-dark conditions. Some of these conditions were externally motivated by the media, race relations, and history, and others were self-inflicted. These conditions were confusing, degrading, and just plain frightening.

There is a need to go back, as the old folks used to say, to the old landmarks. There is a need to go back to the way things were years ago when there was respect and dignity for one another, where parents held a high place in the order, and where teachers were revered and looked up to as the cream of the society's crop. Where kids were required to be in before the sun goes down. Where young people said "Yes, ma'am" and "Yes, sir" to those considered adults. Where did we go wrong? Somewhere we lost our way to the light switch.

Years ago, we looked forward to a simple cone of ice cream, a butter cookie, or a MoonPie . A time when kids would get pleasure from squirting each other with the water hose; when sitting down for a game of dominos or checkers was a way to relax; when playing a game of marbles and hopscotch was something to look forward to; when our primary toys were a rickrack, a yo-yo, or a bicycle; and when simply making and flying a kite was something to look forward to. When did we slip on the banana peel? We lost our way to the light switch.

Our young men, particularly, could stand an old-fashioned butt-whipping from mamas and grandmothers from past generations. Don't you agree? I don't know about you, but those women of experience (you notice that I didn't say *old*) didn't take any mess. If you were brave enough to talk back to them, it was understood that you would, without a doubt, suffer the consequences. Those consequences could run the gamut of picking a few teeth off the floor from a backhand to the mouth or being banished to the darkest part of the house for the rest of your young life with the only nourishment being bread and water. Maybe it was just simply getting it over by being taken to the woodshed. If you survived, the lesson was learned, and though we would do other mischievous things, that particular one would not be repeated until the blisters healed.

Though all of our collective ideas and knowledge will not immediately switch the light on and move us from the darkness into the marvelous light, it will go a long way in publicizing the issue and devising a plan of exit. The method involves education, knowledge, leadership, honesty, integrity, dependability, spirituality, and work ethic, and comes with love, sacrifice, patience, involvement, and toughness. You can surely take that to the bank.

In the work that follows, I want to introduce you to AJ, a young man who lost his way to the light switch. He had everything going for himself, but what follows in this young man's life shows how important it is to come out of the dark into the marvelous light. This is his story.

CHAPTER I

Things Aren't Always as They Seem

The opportunity to practice brotherhood presents itself every time you meet a human being.

— *Jane Wyman*

In Chicago, the Windy City, a place where the winters are bone-chillingly cold, the snow has a majestic sense about it as it glistens in the evening sunlight. The air that you breathe seem to freeze and crumble before your very eyes. To venture out without gloves or a scarf to cover your face would mean a red nose and blue fingertips. As the days wore on and the traffic blackened the snow piles lining the avenues and streets of Chicago and filth mixes with the snow runoff creating a muddy and dismal version of it's a dark, dark world, this is the Picasso that is painted. The summers are hot and muggy as a steam room and much too short. Just walking swiftly in the humidity of the summers here in Chicago creates a sauna-like environment that makes whatever you are wearing wet and uncomfortable. But this is my city, and the love it with all of its flaws, scratches, and warts on its underbelly.

I grew up on the south side of Chicago, the Washington Park area, better known as the ghetto . In society's mind, ghettos were low-income areas with high incidents of crime and severe poverty, but it was much more than that. It housed some of the most talented and misunderstood individuals, who, if given the opportunity, could make significant impact on every aspect of society. Some people are born with silver spoons in their mouths, while others have toothpicks. I can still taste the wood from the toothpick, so you know I had no silver spoon in my mouth or even in the kitchen drawers.

The slums were even worse than ghettos because generally, over half of the community lives off welfare and crime is part of the daily smorgasbord. The police tend to stay away from the slums unless they are looking for a reason to use excessive force. Even cab drivers have limits to their lines of demarcation. There are just some places that are not worth risking your life over. There were places like Altegold Gardens in Riverdale, where run-down low income projects and abandon buildings stand as painful reminders of a hopeless people. Cabrini Green on the north side, where drive-by shootings were not the exception but the rule, even made the cab drivers nervous to venture into the space. Why we take our feelings of hopelessness out on each other, I will never understand.

Things were tough for lower-middle-class families like mine. I define our condition as lower-middle class because we were not dirt poor but we couldn't buy things that we wanted and had to settle for the things we needed. Looking forward to a tax return was mostly an exercise in futility. We were closer to the have-nots versus the haves, if you know what I mean. There were few, if any, white slums, and even the Hispanic neighborhoods were mostly working-class folks with decent jobs. All of the worst parts of Chicago were over 95 percent African American and Latino. In places like Englewood, Fuller Park, Woodlawn, North Lawndale, Grand Boulevard, and Riverdale, it seemed that over half the population in these areas lived off welfare or other government assistance programs. It was not because they wanted to, but that's the hand that they were dealt.

Some self-proclaimed economic brain-e-acts, who didn't know crap about how we survived from check to check, would say that we should "pull ourselves up by our own bootstraps," but some of these particular boots were strapless, if you get my drift. It's easy to generalize and say that folks should be able to get themselves out of poverty, but so many became victims of their environment. Not much required, not much desired. Poverty in these streets seem to be handed down from generation to generation. Something or someone has to break the strangle-hold of poverty on my community.

Gangbanging was a way of life in and around the city that I called home. If you lived in the 79th Street area, it was controlled by a gang called "9". The low end around 53rd and Daman were controlled by the MOEs, and the Hooks and the Westside was dominated by the Vice Lords. No, I was not one of those who sought the gang banger life for security, though it crossed my mind more than a time or two. Anyone who couldn't see that gangs were a losing proposition must have been stuck on stupid. Every week, the meat wagon was hauling away another casualty of the street war that became a way of life in my ghetto. Don't underestimate the attraction of gangs because if you truly look at their structure, much can be learned from it. They have a strong operational governance process or operating structure. They are well disciplined, dedicated to their vision and have a solid infrastructure. Young people are drawn to them because of what they offer verses what they are getting from their own families. There is caring, responsibility, structure, income, food, reward and coaching. No I am not glorifying gangs by any means but I am simply asking that we not underestimate the solid structure that exists.

I have seen them as young as elementary school, sucking the earth before they had a chance to learn their multiplication tables or how to structure a sentence. Many of the mothers who grieved for them were, in more cases than not, still children themselves. I was determined that my little sister would not end up that way. Some of the caskets were no bigger than an oversized cooler. It was not unusual to find Glock-22c's,

GSG-5s, 357s, or 45s tucked in book bags and lockers in elementary and middle schools, when many of these kids should have been enjoying just being a kid and in school learning history, English, math, etc . Instead, they were learning how to survive on the unforgiving streets of Chi Town. Guns and drugs were as easy to get as stealing an orange from the local street vendors. Just walking down the side streets and allies in "ghetto hell," the pushers would be selling their products, ranging from designer clothes to designer drugs and sophisticated automatic weapons.

During the warmer weather, if you wanted to check out the honeys, you would clean up your ride, put a good spit shine on the 22s, and head for Rainbow Beach, Hood Beach, Private Beach, or the Point. Man, some of these sisters had no right to be so fine. String bikinis ought to be outlawed because the eyes are not designed to take the kind of punishment dished out by some of these Chicago honeys. Some women should have to audition for permission to wear some of the outfits that are on display at the beach fashion show. They truly give rise to the meaning of fun in the sun.

When a woman starts approaching 175 pounds, it behooves her to cover that big ass with a tablecloth or something. Man, some of those big girls have no shame. I bet it takes them half a day to find that string once it is consumed by their hippo-like rear ends. Man, a brother had to be on his p's and q's with these fine hammas, or they would henpeck a brother into thinking he is all of that when actually, they were spinning that web of deceit to wipe a brother out. If you spend too much time on the body and not evaluate the mind, these sisters will make a brother think he is king when he is only a jack.

The drug running through the veins of those living in the many ghettos of Chicago is called poverty. The halfway houses were filled with people who were bankers, lawyers, business owners, and professors at some time in their lives, but a single miscalculation, a bad decision, or a mis-calibrated investment had sent them into a spiral of misfortune and depression. You can bet that drugs were somewhere in the mix. Drugs don't care what socio-economic status you occupy. If you are weak enough to fall under its spell, it will own your heart, mind and pocketbook.

When people lose hope, it becomes easy to get lost in the temporary relief of dope. What they fail to realize is that on the other side of that false high is an even greater and deeper low. At the end of each needle was an arm attached to a problem. Hope is an effective weapon against poverty because it gives you the strength to continually get up and shake off the dirt from the fall. Don't believe that getting up is easy, the hardest part is not falling in the first place.

Like many other families, my folks were struggling day to day to just make ends meet. They made some decent money, but it wasn't mine. My mama would slide me a twenty spot here and there, but I didn't feel very good about it. I wanted to be in a position to take care of her someday because Lord knows that she sacrificed so much for us on a daily basis. My pops didn't control the money in our house, even though he was lead to believe that he did. It was useless to ask him for anything because we knew the answer would be no primarily because he also didn't have much. He had as much dust in his pockets as we did. The dude worked his ass off and brought every cent home to moms and that says a lot about their relationship. I have to give them their due because they would always have food on the table and clothes on our backs, which was more than many who suffered through this war of poverty. People were freaking out over making sixty and seventy thousand big ones, which I didn't understand because my mind was stretched out on the Oprah- and Tiger Woodstype cash.

My Parents were semi-religious which means that they believed in a higher power but there were limits to how much time they were willing to spend at church and they knew as I do that many of these so called preachers were nothing more than con men who just walked into the pulpit because they had a gift of gab and were not called by God to preach any more than I was. I believe in God but know that man has put his sticky fingers on the Bible which makes it an imperfect document. Religion, to a degree has crippled our people because they totally follow their so called religion and stop thinking for themselves. Now don't get me wrong, I am not against anyone who choose that route. I won't try to change you and I hope you don't try to change me.

Selling drugs was the means to an end for a lot of folks who had a death wish, but I couldn't cross that line, big money or not. I saw what drugs did to those close to me and around me, and I was determined not to be controlled by anything or anybody but me. Life was hard enough without waking up every day having to dig out from not only your condition but also your habits. After seeing my uncle Richie go from being one of the sharpest, best dressed analysts on Wall Street to a halfway house, had convinced me that taking the high road made more sense. This dude, at one time, drove around in a steel-gray Porsche and wore the finest of Ferragamo shoes especially designed and cut for him in New York City. I swear his suits were cut especially for him because of the way they fitted his well chiseled body. Man if I didn't know better, I would think that they were imported from a country like Italy or somewhere. Uncle Richie had class and was always seen with some of the finest arm candy in Chicago. They were not just pretty faces looking for a way out of a dismal situation, but instead were from MIT, Harvard, Yale, Brown, and other rich Ivy League institutions and they were not all black. Now just a shell of a man confined to a wheelchair, Uncle Richie spends his days staring out of an open window and hasn't spoken a word for years. I guess the stress of losing his fortune and losing his status was too much to bare. A bad investment, loans to family, and the high life had broken this icon of a man. Life had taken his will. When hope is gone, drugs seem to temporarily ease the pain.

Tracks littered the arms of the young and old, the clean and the unclean, white and black, rich and poor. Drugs became a means to an end for many who gave up hope for dope. The real money was not made by those who sold the drugs but by those outside who were capitalizing on the hopelessness and mental weakness of the least, the last, and the lost. The real losers were a generation of young brothers who became pawns and runners for the scumbags who lured them with money and hope but only gave them crack and a drug habit that started a life spiral that would have little chance of return.

Drugs did not originate in the slums of Chicago, but it definitely thrived there, as it did in many low-income parts of many neighborhoods in the cities. You name it—it was available on the street. Anyone could get guns, marijuana, cocaine, uppers, downers, and the universal drug of choice—alcohol. The cops knew that this poison and hopelessness was everywhere and chose to simply look the other way. Some even capitalized on the flow of dirty money into our neighborhoods by making their late-night visits with their hands out for kickbacks. The drug money greased the pockets of some of the most powerful people in Chicago. In the areas most of us considered to be across the tracks, the local officials were content to let us kill, steal, rob, and shoot up as long as we paid our block fees and kept away from their neighborhoods.

Yes, the haves and have-nots does exist and drugs and prostitution flowing through our neighborhoods would delay any attempt to change the distructive direction that was eating a hole in our souls.

CHAPTER II

I Am Who I Am

Excuse me. I am so caught up in my personal plight and the sad state of affairs around me that I totally forgot to introduce myself. My name is AJ, and I want you to remember that. AJ stands for August James. Why my parents would name me after one of the months of the year, I do not know. Maybe it was because the month of August is named for the Roman emperor Augustus. Augustus was a bad dude, so that's got to be the reason. As macho as I claim to be, I can't understand why I am afraid of the dark. It's something about darkness that gives me a feeling of being trapped. Now that's my story, and I am sticking to it.

I was the older of two children born to my parents. The other was a downright fox of a sister named Chantal. She had honey-brown hair that flowed like a cool, quiet stream on a summer day. Her eyes were as brown as her hair, and she was gifted with the brains that I could only wish for. There were a lot of years between us, but she was my heart and soul. Anyone who had a desire to bite a piece of that pie better know that I will be watching.

Man, I dreaded the day that some dude was going to come to our front door trying to push up on her, because if he did, he was going to have me to deal with, and that's a fact. My conscience was bothering me because I knew how I was, and I knew these hard legs from all over town would be licking their chops to get at Chantal. I was the focus of many a dude who knew I had my eyes on their sisters, just as I feared would happen to Chantal now. Just thinking about her brings a smile to my face. Everything about her was close to perfection. The way she walked, talked and smelled let you know that she was going to be special.

I was the child that every parent wanted but soon wanted to forget. My folks tried their best to bring me up right and place me in the right schools, but I had rejected their attempt to make me one of the preppy "wootzies" that walk around with their sweaters around their necks, a Timex watch, an array of Dockers in their closets, and at least two pairs of penny loafers stuck under their beds. I was determined to do it my way. I stopped short of having my pants hanging half off my butt, but all of the other teenage traits were definitely in my portfolio. Chugging beer, smoking a joint, staying out all night, and putting a notch in my belt for every pair of legs that was caught on my joystick was my legacy. All of us who grew up in the stiffening grip of poverty did our share of shoplifting, stealing from the local fruit stands, and tossing a brick through a neighbor's window, but we controlled our streets. Poverty did not remove the respect that people had for the older members of the community. Even Ned the Wino said "Yes, sir" and "Yes, ma'am" to the patriarchs and matriarchs on the block.

My folks were hardworking people, but the pressures of making ends meet were too much. They eventually tried to solve their problems at the bottom of a Crown Royal bottle. As bad as that might seem, they were not the hard-core element that consumed cough syrup, took uppers or downers, or had tracks in their arms just to ease the pain of hopelessness. They had tried and tried to do it the old American way, but that same American way kept slapping them in the behind. Every time they took a step forward, there were two steps backward waiting to smack a hickey on their asses. After Uncle Sam got his piece and the bills were paid, there was little left to do other things, like get a better TV or have more than one pair of sneaks under my bed. We always had food in the cabinet though Moms would burn water. She was a gorgeous woman but God did not gift her with the ability to follow a recipe. It was dangerous having Moms anywhere near a stove. Mom was such a catch that my dad didn't care about her culinary skills, I am sure she made up for it in other ways.

My pops was an easygoing, passive type who had to get pissed off before he would come close to raising his voice. That was fine with me because I didn't want to hear that lip flapping anyway. My mom had finished her degree in marketing from the University of Chicago, Midway, while Pops spent four years at Indiana University where he received a bachelor's degree in business administration. What had happened to my parents had caused me to place limited value on what an education could do for me. Life gets you to a point where you start to doubt whether things will ever get better, and once that happens, hell . . . It's got you. Life is what you make it, not what it makes you. It was a lesson that came hard to me.

After years of me watching my folks fall down, get up, and fall down again, they resorted to running from their problems and throwing down liquor like it was water. I tried the wine and liquor scene myself, but it didn't fit my social appetite and quite honestly, was a waste of good grapes. Riding the white horse (cocaine) was not my thang either, but I have to admit I did dabble in the hallucinating weed from time to time. It gave me a sense of calm that usually eludes me as I sought my daily dose of sanity in the streets of ghetto hell. Man this weed will one day be accepted as more of a positive than a negative. The way it makes you feel has to have some healing values.

This part of Chicago that time seems to have forgotten may have been where I started, but it was not where I planned to finish, and you can take that to the bank 'cause it's money. The Windy City had become a curse for richly talented and naive opportunists like me. The streets had claimed many a good man from living beyond their means, trying to satisfy women who preyed on the weak-minded and those they thought to have deep pockets. These cougars and bear-rillas drained them dry and left them cold and angry at the world for allowing themselves to be suckered like mice in a trap. When they finally did come to their senses, their cars and homes were repossessed and their bank accounts were so low that there was not a need to even get a monthly statement. Now that's low. Many had only enough money left in their accounts to keep it open.

I was an average student in high school. I made B's without even trying. All of the teachers tried their best to get me to realize my potential but AJ was determined to find his own way. Popularity with the fine young things was what motivated me. I knew I could have been the big man on campus for playing baseball, football or basketball but that was a waste of my time. Though I dabbled in the sports and was pretty good to, it was not my focus. If I had to pick a favorite pastime, it would be basketball because I was silky smooth when I applied my skills. Without trying, I was better than most of the jocks on our teams and the coaches knew it. Academically, numbers came easy to me but I wasn't interested. History and geography seemed a waste because I didn't see the value in looking back. I wasted a lot of precious time in high school not knowing that it would affect by brand in negative ways.

After finishing high school, I was lucky enough to have been offered a scholarship for athletics at UCLA and Northwestern. I was not as naturally smart as Chantal, but what I lacked in brain power, I made up for in hard-line bullshit and street savvy. I was primarily bored throughout my high school experience because things came pretty easy to me, and I was able to charm my way through the early grades. I was semi-smart but lazy, creative but lacked motivation. Grades were not that hard to come by, but they were less important to me than those stone-cold Michael Jordan moves on the B-ball court.

Call it what you want but I started to realize that B-ball was money and plenty of it, and I was about getting my share. I wanted to one day be able to drop a cool hundred in old homeless Jake's pencil cup on the corner of third and Main. Right now, based on the cobwebs in my pockets, I need to be nuzzling up to old Jake and holding a cup or something myself. I didn't have a pot to piss in or a window to throw it out of. They say that the almighty dollar is the root of all evil, but let me have some evil. Going to school, macking girls, having your own crib, paying bills, and keeping petro in the ride require some of that evil, and I was all about getting my share no matter the consequences.

I finished high school with a respectable grade point average, and my basketball skills were enough to get me into Northwestern. I knew then that I was wasting my time, but I was tired of hearing Mom's mouth because of her and Pops having finished college. There were many days that our conversations got downright combative. I remember this one day that I walked in the house expecting a little peace and quiet when Moms just couldn't resist pulling my chain, and the sparks started to fly. "AJ, have you been down to school to check on those transcripts?"

"No, Moms, but I will when I get time, so quit trippin'."

"AJ, I swear you are one lazy soul. How you figure to get a good job if you don't get into college? And how can you get in college if you don't get that registration finished?"

"Moms, you are talking smack 'cause both you and Pops finished, and look what it's gotten you."

The next thing I knew, I was picking myself up off the floor. "Boy, I brought you into this world, and I will take you out if you think you can stand here and disrespect me like that. Your father and I may not have much, but we work hard to make ends meet around here. You got food on the table, the lights are on, and you have clothes on your trifling behind and even a little spending change. And we have to sit here and listen to your crap! Where did it all come from? Certainly not from the sweat off your lazy behind."

At that time, looking up from the floor, I then realized that moms was right. I was being trifling and disrespectful and deserved the slap down that I had just gotten. I could see the hurt in her eyes and I was the cause. Moms truly loved me, and I knew it and it was the first time I had ever seen her lose it like that. Man, I struck a nerve that I never want to ever strike again. Pops just stood there, shaking his head. "Boy, you know you deserved that, and as long as you are in this house, you will respect your mother and me. If you feel like you can't do that, then you know what you have to do. And understand, before you make the wrong decision and walk out of here without apologizing, once you leave, there is no coming back."

Pops was a man of few words, but when he did speak, you knew he was serious. Man, I wanted to walk out right then and never come back, but common sense told me that they were right, and it would still be a while before my walking away would be permanent. I knew that I had to go to school or be doomed to this environment for the duration, and that wasn't even an option. I swallowed my pride and apologized to moms, not because I was afraid of pops but because he was right.

That verbal scolding didn't feel good, but it hit home with me, and it would be the last time I put myself or my parents through that. I was still sitting on the floor with my arms around my knees, still smarting from the Hurricane Katrina–like tongue-lashing. I looked up into their faces and felt like hell because they were right. I was being a son of a B, and everyone knew it. As Moms and Pops turned to walk away, I said in a trembling voice, "Mom, I am so sorry for what I said, and I truly didn't mean it. I was just being stupid, and I am so sorry. If you guys want me to leave, I will? " They turned around and just stared at me but didn't say a word. I knew they didn't want me to leave, but I didn't know what else to say.

That evening, I casually made it down to the registration office to finish my papers and get a list of my classes for the upcoming school term. Even though UCLA was very attractive and would have made it possible for me to play in a premier basketball program, Chicago was home, and all of my homeboys, and particularly the ladies, could not survive without old AJ being on the scene.

I had to do the school thing to satisfy my folks and to get the mad money that I needed. Most of my road dogs were hanging on the corners, smoking weed, telling lies, and watching big-ass women walk by. Most of them had no ambition, and college was out of the question, though many of them had more smarts than I could ever be capable of, I grudgingly admit. Many of these dudes could talk Wall Street with the best of them and kept current on what was going on politically but felt that a formal education was not in their DNA. I started to realize that if I didn't get registered, I would have to battle with Uncle Sam and that wasn't going to happen. I didn't lose anything in this man's army.

The day had come for final registration, and I had decided to ask Moms to go with me, hoping that she would have sobered up from the scolding high I had placed her on. I walked to her bedroom door and asked, "Moms, would you mind going with me to get the final registration done?" She had me on the silent treatment for a few days, so I didn't know what to expect. She turned and looked me squarely in the eyes as only a mother can do, and I couldn't help but drop my head.

"AJ, yes, I will go with you, but I must be back before 4:00 p.m. I have to get down to the salon because I have two good customers that I have to squeeze in today."

"OK, most stuff is done. I just have to go to the bursar's office to pay my tuition."

It was necessary to have her go with me because the initial jack had to be put down on my courses, and I had nothing in my pockets but little balls of paper from the washing machine. You know how the paper in your pants rolls into lint balls in your pockets when the pants go through the washing machine. Moms and I headed to the carport to get into my ride. As I started to get in on the driver's side, I noticed that Moms was looking at me and still standing on the passenger side with her arms folded. "What?" I said.

"AJ, get your good-for-nothing butt out of that car and come and open my door. I am going to teach you some manners if it kills me."

"My bad, Moms, you know you raised a gentleman. All the ladies tell me that."

"If they call you a gentleman, then I question their ' Lady' title."

It was now approaching noontime, and I wanted to get this over with. The registration lines were long, and I wasn't one with a lot of patience. As I stood in line, waiting my turn to get to the registration window, I couldn't help wondering if the honeys were as cute as some that I had seen. If so, then this could be a very productive and rewarding experience. Just as I leaned against the wall to take a little of the load off, this perfect ten walked by and went straight into the office. I couldn't help following the motion of that ocean 'cause she had curves in places that other girls didn't have places.

"AJ, keep your mind on what you are here for and off that girl's butt."

"Mom, please chill. You know Pops was peeping on your attributes too when you were in college, and I have to admit I don't blame him a bit."

"Boy, you better hush. I'm your mother, and my attributes are none of your concern. Is that all you men think about?"

"No, not all, but most," I said with a smile. "Ain't nothing like getting that honey from the beehive and hope not to get stung."

"AJ, you are a heathen, and stop saying *ain't*. It's like you don't have any home training. I hate to say it—standing in this line is most likely a waste of time, but you are going to school, boy," she said as she reached up and gave me a playful slap on the back of my head. "You have no respect saying that stuff in front of me."

I reached out and grabbed her and gave her a hug, which brought out the most beautiful smile. I knew how to get to moms. She loves me, and that was no question. I appreciated it though I didn't know how to show it most of the time. "August James, put me down boy. You are just like your daddy, you think all you guys have to do is strong arm women and we will melt in your hands. Well this woman is not a push over and you know that by now, so PUT ME DOWN"

Just as quickly as she had appeared, the honey that glided by us a few minutes before made a return trip. "Mama, watch this. Let me show you how bad your son is. Watch, she will walk by, then stop and give me that sexy look and play the hard card, then give me those digits. If she does that, I got her. Now watch the champ go to work."

"Hey there, girl. My name is AJ, what's yours?"

She walked a few steps past us, stopped, turned around, and said, "Hay is for horses, and I know you can come up with something better than that. It's Tanya and not *girl*."

"I stand corrected, Ms. Tanya. Tanya, meet my mother, Rachael James."

"Pleased to meet you, Mrs. James. I know you taught him better than that." As she turned to leave, she said, "Mrs. James, it was indeed a pleasure meeting you, in spite of your lame offspring. You are a classy lady, I can tell. I hope some of it will eventually rub off, if you know what I mean."

They gave each other a high five, and Tanya was off with an extra swing of the hips and a sassy smile as she slid away with a final "Good-bye to you too, boy."

"I got your boy right—"

Before I could finish, Moms popped me again. "AJ, that's what I am talking about. That mouth of yours needs some Clorox."

"But Moms, I can't let her front on a brother like that, and you giving her a high five and all."

Moms covered her mouth to keep from laughing out loud. Then, without even thinking about it, she said, "You go, girl."

I couldn't believe that I had been played in front of my moms. "Moms, chill with that."

"AJ, what champ? You must have meant *chump*. Any self-respecting woman wouldn't respond to that weak line you just laid on Tanya," said Rachael. "She seemed to be a nice and respectful girl, and it seems you can learn a thing or two from her. Actually, AJ, that's an example of you thinking with the wrong head, my young Nubian offspring. Now put your loins back in your pants and get up to that window and register."

To say the least, I was embarrassed because that had always worked until now. Tanya must know that there will be a payday in the offing. I will hunt her ass down and prove to her that I am nobody's whipping post. Nobody disses old AJ without getting something in return.

Moms wanted to escort me to school on the first day, but there was no way I was having that. That's the ultimate embarrassment—having your moms show up like she did when you were in elementary school. My first day on campus was uneventful. It consisted of brief visits to each class on the schedule, a visit to the bookstore, and on to the cafeteria. As I strolled into Smith Hall where the cafeteria was located, I looked around as if I were a tourist in New York City. There were students everywhere, none of which were familiar to me. These faces were light-years away from Pookie, Cat Daddy, and Maurice, my closest acquaintances. I wasn't feeling like conversation, so I got a sandwich and a soda and went to the farthest end of the cafeteria, where there were many empty tables.

It was fun people watching, and I have to admit that there were some well-structured women walking around. It was like the United Nations, women of every color and size. Just as I stood to get rid of my trash, a voice came from behind me. "Hey, boy, I mean AJ. How are you?" As I turned to return the sentiment, I saw that it was Tanya, grinning and skinning because she had fronted a brother. I just stood staring at her, and she knew why. With a big smile, she said, "AJ, no hard feelings about the other day, right?"

"Wrong, my sarcastic and not-so-funny sister, you don't get off that easy. You made a brother look bad in front of his moms, and I won't forget that. You can believe that."

"AJ, you brought that on yourself, and you know it."

Man, this girl had an edge about her that pissed me off but was drawing me to her at the same time. "The way you approached me in front of your mother was wack and you know it. No woman wants to be addressed as 'hay girl'!" I will be in the cafeteria around this time every day, so if you want to have lunch and talk, I am available."

I was standing there virtually in shock. No woman has ever been so aggressive toward me, and I didn't quite know how to deal with it. "That's cool, Tanya, take care." I left her standing and watching my back as I walked away.

A few days later, I saw Tanya walking hand-in-hand with an East Indian guy. I didn't even know this lady, but I was feeling cheated on. I followed them for a few minutes, long enough to see him give her a kiss as they went separate ways. I hurried to catch her before she went to class. "Tanya, . . . Hey, hey, Tanya . . . Wait up."

"Oh, hi, boy," said Tanya with a mischievous grin. "How are things with you? How are your classes going?"

"Now you got to cut that 'boy' shit, Tanya—enough is enough. As to your question, the classes are fine. What about yours?"

"Everything is cool with me also. So you're talking to me again," she said with a smile.

"Yes, I'm cool as long as you cut out that 'boy' shit. I couldn't help but notice the guy you were walking with. Is that your . . ."

Before I could get it out, Tanya said, "Oh, that was Rahem, my husband."

"Tanya, you're married?"

"Yes, I am, and happily. Is that a surprise?"

"I have to admit that it is, because I thought . . ."

"You thought what, that I would fall for that weak line of yours and that I was available? AJ, first of all, you are not my type, and secondly, Rahem and I have a daughter. We are both here to finish our doctoral programs—him in medicine and me in finance. Guys like you are simply pretty faces and are often empty on the inside. Not trying to hurt your feelings, but I call them like I see them. You seem to be a nice guy, AJ, but I can already tell that you lack focus. We can be friends, but that has to include Rahem. I have to go, must meet a friend at the library."

I had been fried, dyed, and laid to the side, and there was nothing I could do about it. I had indeed met my match. In fact, she was more than a match for me, and even if she had been single, I am afraid that she wouldn't have found her way into my little black book. What I did realize was that she was the standard that I eventually aspired to have as a companion. I was impressed, as well as disappointed. What continues to stick in my craw is her saying that I wasn't her type. I agree with her about the pretty face thing, but *what* type am I? If this was the treatment that I am to receive from these ladies here on campus, this was going to be a long semester. Talk about bringing a brother back to earth, DAM! From this confrontation with Tanya, it brought to mind something that General Colin Powel had said. I was something like, "you had to consider the persons that you are keeping close to you and purge those who are not going in the same direction that you are." Not exactly his words but the meaning is close enough. That may be something to consider since I had, in one day, been slapped down and embarrassed all in the course of a 24 hour period.

I once again turned my attention to the basketball court. Married or not, sooner or later, Tanya will have to tell me what she meant about not being her type. I guess she likes guys with all brain and no game. But it also seemed that the old game of mine needed a bit of polishing. It reminded me about the old saying that, "no matter how good you think you are, there is always someone standing in the wings that's better". Tanya was better, a lot better so back to the drawing board for old AJ.

CHAPTER III

The Beginning of Basketball Season

The streets of Chicago produced dudes who could compete with the best minds on the planet, play B-ball at the Michael Jordan level, and totally crush a dude on the football field. Instead, most of them ended up like OJ Simpson, with numbers on the front of their uniforms instead of the back. If the military didn't get them, the drugs usually would.

Balling came naturally to many of us in the hood. Being the starting forward on the varsity basketball team at Northwestern, I found that hoops were easy to me, as was attracting the attention of the cream of the crop of fine women on campus and the pro scouts who would show up every now and then. At six feet two inches and averaging a respectable twenty-eight points, ten rebounds, and eight steals per game, I was a pretty hot ticket on the pro scout's notebook from the very beginning. Coach kept telling me to put some meat on my narrow ass because the big forwards would eat me alive. I like my skinny ass because it allowed me to fit in tight spots, if you know what I mean.

My pops always told us that everyone was just one bad situation away from the soup line. The older I got, the more I understood what he meant. Many of the halfway houses were filled with doctors, lawyers, and businessmen who had the world on a string but through sheer bad luck or a misplaced or ill-advised decision, had found themselves living in hopelessness and despair. We have to be careful about the people we step on as we head for the top because we may see them again and we head for the bottom. This was my turning point and for the first time, I was concerned about my future. How long would that feeling last.

The coach at Northwestern, "Big House" Boyd, took a special interest in me primarily because of my skills, but I must have taken a few years off of his life because of my lack of a solid work ethic. He was called Big House because the arena at Northwestern was huge, and he was an imposing figure. He stood six feet five inches tall with his plaid bow tie, suspenders, and a cigar that was never lit and hung from a mouth that seemed to stretch from one ear to another. He had a voice that pierced the heavy air of the gym like a hot knife through butter. I have yet to see anyone push up against Big House. They knew better. The dude had arms like tree trunks, and you just had to look at a brother and you knew that you were in his house and to come right or suffer the consequences.

When you think of someone called Big House, you automatically think of a large, imposing black dude, but this Big House was as white as the sheets on my bed and could knock a hole in a brick wall. He was responsible for more dudes going to the NBA than any other college coach except John Wooden at UCLA. Big House thought that with enough coaching and counseling, he could make me a model citizen. What he didn't know was that I could take the game or leave it. I wanted the glory of what the game could do for me financially, but those hard two-hour practices and sweating until I was exhausted from the suicide sprints and jumping jacks wasn't the way I wanted to spend my evenings. I was constantly late for practices, showed little interest in the film sessions prior to games, and my arrogance surprised even me at times.

I was out of shape, and I knew it, the coach knew it, and my teammates knew it. I was either going to make this a serious attempt at basketball or call it quits. I was talented and gifted but severely unfocused and naive to the politics of success, and I enjoyed smoking a little gitty-up weed at times. It cleared old AJ's head and made me think clearly. I should have been thrown off the team a long time ago, but Coach Boyd had this soft spot for me which I never appreciated. He would say, "AJ, you are a waste of two legs and balls. I am wasting my time thinking that you will ever amount to anything. I don't know why I waste my time." Maybe he was right. But like my parents, he wanted something for me that I didn't seem to want for myself.

In our first scrimmage game with the University of Wisconsin, I stunk up the place with poor shooting and even worse defense. It was the first time that I had heard boos in my career, and it didn't feel good. I had a reputation to uphold. If I couldn't play any better than this in the next game, I might as well pack it in, and you know old AJ ain't no quitter. So I knew what I had to do. I arranged with the Janitor a little extra practice time after hours. Mr. Freeman was a good man. He had been the janitor at Northwestern for over 20 years and is well respected by everyone in the administration. "Mr Freeman, I need a favor. I am crashing and burning out on the court and unless I turn this thing around quickly, I am going to be kicked off the team by Big House". "Listen AJ, we both know that it's against administrations rules but what they don't know won't hurt them. I have to have the lights on anyway so it's not costing them anything. I will give you one and a half hours and I will shut things down O.K. When I say let's go, pack it up". "You are the best Mr. Freeman, I got you," said AJ. The next practice, I was there before the rest, taking free throws and doing wind sprints. When Coach got there, I had already worked up a big sweat and was eager to start the shoot-around.

When the coach approached me with this look of disbelief in his big bloodshot eyes, all I could say was "What?"

"AJ, are you okay? What's going on? You never show up on time and not warmed up . Don't get me wrong, I have been waiting on this for a long time, so what gives?"

"Coach, can you do me a favor and allow me to speak to the team before we start?"

"All right, AJ, what's the deal here?"

"Coach, just trust me this one time."

"All right, AJ, but this had better be good."

I grabbed a basketball to put in my hand because it tends to put me at ease. I looked around the group of guys and made eye contact with each of them before starting. "Listen, guys, I'm not good at this, but I want to sincerely apologize to all of you for not giving it my best against Wisconsin. I let the school down, you down, I let the coach down, and above all, I let myself down. I promise never to allow that to happen again. I appreciate the coach for putting up with me and my attitude over the last few months. The coach should have kicked me off the team, but for whatever his reason, he didn't. He gave me the chance that I needed to see if I could help the team. If you guys don't want me around, I understand, but I really do love playing on this team with you guys, and if you give me another chance, I won't let you down."

Bo Dickey, an all-American point guard spoke up. "AJ, as far as I am concerned, you don't deserve another chance. We have put up with your mess since the beginning of the season because you are a good player, but no more. This little display of seriousness is a show, and I don't believe one bit of it. There are a lot of good players on this team that care about winning and are not as selfish as you are." From that point, I heard a lot of "That's right" and "Yeah " coming from the peanut gallery, which told me that I was not going to be supported anymore by these guys.

Just as I turned to walk away, I heard Coach say, "I know I am not hearing what I think I heard. Bo, of all people, you should be willing to give someone a second chance. After all, I bailed your tail out of being suspended for low grades, didn't I?"

With a bowed head, Bo said, "Yes, Coach."

The coach went on. "Some of you others, like Sam and Ron . . . Didn't you get a second chance when you were accused of breaking into the women's dorm? Even though no harm was done, you both faced suspension until my coaches got involved and pleaded with the chancellor to give your butts another shot. I am very disappointed in all of you, including you, AJ. I have favored you during times when I should have kicked your butt off the team. I saw something in you that even you didn't see in yourself. There is no *I* in *team*, and from this point forward, I will be the only one to use *I* in a sentence. Do all of you understand? AJ is still our team member until I say differently, so if some of you have a problem with that, then you have the right to walk right now." The gym fell silent, and no one dared move an inch. The silence seemed to last, ten minutes when it actually was only a few seconds before Coach said, "All right then, let's get to work and prepare to kick some Ohio butt next week."

Believe me, it was the best thing that could have happened to me. Basketball was important to me, and it had begun to change my attitude about my classes as well. I was back on the right track. We all need a little kick in the tail at some point. For some unknown reason, I was being given a second chance, and I wasn't about to throw it away. In the next game with Ohio State University, I was my old self again. Though I didn't try to score much in that game, I played a smothering defense and had nine steals and fourteen rebounds. I wanted to show the team that I was a complete player and not just a scorer. The next three games, with my team again solidly behind me, I averaged a respectable eighteen points, eight rebounds, and six steals per game. Coach had such a big grin on his face that several times he dropped that huge cigar from his lips, which had never happened before. I was once again back on track, but for how long?

After the game, I was on a natural high and feeling good about myself again. As I walked toward the library, a familiar voice called out to me. "AJ . . . AJ . . . Wait up, I want you to meet Rahem, my husband."

Quite honestly, I had no desire to meet this guy. "Oh, hi, Tanya."

"Rahem, this is AJ. AJ, meet Rahem."

"Hi, Rahem, good to meet you."

"Rahem, AJ was trying to hit on a sister, but I have my arm candy right here." She reached up and gave him a very tender kiss on the cheek.

"Rahem, Tanya is trippin'. You have a lovely wife, but I was not hitting on her." "AJ, don't be embarrassed but you know you are lying and the truth ain't in you. A sister trumped your P-L-A-Y-E-R card and you are fronting to mahe Rahem feel that you weren't hitting on me. My boo is a cool B-r-a-t-h-a and he is secure in this relationship. You didn't know I was married so no harm done.

"AJ, it's good to finally meet you. Tanya told me about you. Don't feel bad, bro, all the guys hit on my Tanya. She is indeed a piece of heaven's pie.

"Look babe, I have to run. So nice meeting you, AJ, and I will see you at home, my love."

I stood watching Rahem disappear between the buildings. I turned to Tanya. "Why did you tell him that I was hitting on you?"

"Why not, AJ? I have nothing to hide. You know you were hitting on me, that's why you were so shocked when you saw me with Rahem. Rahem and I are comfortable with each other, and he is not the jealous type. He knows that I will be home, just like he said. Are you telling me that if I wasn't married, AJ, that you wouldn't have gone after all of this?" She rubbed her hands from her waist down her hips.

"Tanya, you are nice, but old AJ can do better, my conceited sister."

"AJ, you are a liar, and the truth ain't in you." Tanya started to close the space between us. "If what you say is true, then what's that bulge in your pants?" she said as she turned to leave. I was like a kid who had just been caught with his hand in the cookie jar. All I could do was stand there with my hands covering my rock-hard member. She had done it again. This woman had my number, and she knew it. I had never met anyone who had as much charisma and confidence as Tanya, and I could tell that she was off-limits to me and everyone else . . . except Rahem.

I had to stay away from this man-killer or lose my player card. Not only was she fine as hair on a flea's ass, but the girl had the academic thing down pat too. I found out later that she and Rahem lived in a large estate near the Gold Coast, one of the wealthiest neighborhoods in Chicago. She was right; I wouldn't know what to do if I did have a woman like her. Women like Tanya make the normal players look like amateurs.

From that point on, I made it a point to not hang around the areas where Tanya would be seen. She had my nose so open that you could drive a Mack truck through it. I had decided to focus on my studies, which shocked even me. Focusing was difficult enough with the sights on campus, but I was determined not to let Moms down. Just as things were starting to click in the classroom, my old habits started to surface again.

CHAPTER IV

Reba and Faye

Other than that occasional weed, the one thing on the Northwestern campus that did demanded my attention was a perfect ten named Reba, who had hips that could sink ships. She was tall, quiet, and the envy of every girl on campus because of her academic focus, high moral standards, and that killer body that every guy on the yard wanted but was afraid to try for fear of failure. She must have been the product of a mixed marriage because she had long, wavy black hair, a vanilla-white complexion, and blue eyes that were pleasingly angelic. Just one long stare from that perfect ten could make a brother lose his rocks right there on the spot.

Through all of my hoeing around, I fail to give proper attention to Ashley, my on and off love bunny. Ash, was a very private companion who didn't sweat me for time and attention. She just seem to enjoy what little time we had together. I think we both knew that it was a matter of convenience for the both of us. When we were together, it was nice and without hassle. If I don't see her for days at a time, she is fine with it. I knew at some point that Ash would tire of this arrangement. But I was going to make it last for as long as I could. I loved her but I was not in love with her. I had a hunger for more of a challenge than what

Ash provided so my wondering eyes and loins would continue to seek the female upper crust that I knew was out there.

Though Reba was capable of crossing over at any time because of her looks, it was obvious that she was black through and through. Her walk, her talk, and her attitude let you know that, without a doubt, she was definitely a sister beyond any stretch of the imagination. She did not hang out with the posse after class because she was too busy working on the school's newspaper and spending her life in the library. Reba was unlike the other girls because she covered up all of her goodies. She wore long, flowing skirts and blouses that came to the neck. The girl showed no cleavage at all, but you could tell she had a brick house under that Mormon-looking outfit that she usually wore. Every now and then she would wear something relatively short to her standards, and that's when you knew that she had a diamond under there. I don't know if it was her exotic looks with her long, flowing black hair or her mysterious nature that drove me crazy, but whichever it was, it had put a love-hook in old AJ.

I was once again the hottest thing on the yard because of my basketball skills, and Reba still didn't care if I existed or not. The jocks usually had their way with the women on campus, but getting this one would be tougher than breaking into Fort Knox. I wanted no part of being the hunter because I was already at the top of that game. I wanted to be the hunted and specifically, hunted by the only woman that made me forget the likes of Beyoncé and Janet Jackson. This girl was breaking my cool, and I didn't like it at all.

Many of these flake-heads on the yard thought that Reba was left-handed because they never saw her with any guys on campus. If that were true, then what a waste of good flesh that could be laying right here in the palm of old AJ's hands. I was determined to find out if she was swinging on the pole or licking the mustard jar. I tried everything, from physically bumping into her in the cafeteria to volunteering for work after class in the newspaper office, just to be close enough to strike when the iron was hot. It was like trying to strike gold in a silver mine. I was out of this girl's league, but it wouldn't stop me from taking a shot at her fine ass.

Her ignoring me brought on an obsession that awakened all of the testosterone in my frail body. Every other girl on campus, black or white, practically took off their thongs when I walked by, but not Reba. It was like dangling fresh meat in front of a wild animal, just having that perfect specimen of a woman anywhere within driving distance. Just getting a whiff of her body lotion sent my senses into orbit. Even when she spoke to me in that soft, tantalizing voice, I would go around the corner and bite a hole in my damn lip like some fool instead of just grabbing her in one of AJ's lip-lock specials. I wasn't going to allow any woman to set old AJ on his heels. I was going to be sure that she was receptive before making my patented move. My record was intact on never being refused not counting Tanya, and I wasn't about to have that broken by this perfect ten or anyone else. Tanya didn't count because she is married thank God. She could ruin a brother's reputation as cold blooded as she is. I wasn't about to let any of these man killers derail AJ, YOU CAN BET ON THAT.

On campus, there is a pecking order. There are those who lead and can call their shots and those who follow and are more than willing to take what is left behind by the leaders. Up to now, I was one of the leaders . . . I thought. No matter how good you think you are, there is always one son of a mother who is your nightmare. Shawn Samuels was the one guy on campus that could clean my clock in every sport but basketball, but the white boy was brain dead when it came to the books. He was a tall, lean, athletically built redbone with freckles wrapped around one of the meanest tempers imaginable. We, on occasion, had a few run-ins but nothing serious until now. I was lucky that Shawn chose football over B-ball because I didn't like playing second fiddle to anyone, especially a white boy who tried to identify as black. Though I was nowhere near the physical specimen of Shawn, I was no slouch and didn't back down from any mother's son, and you better believe that. It was not in my DNA to punk out, but the time would come when I should have. It was like prison in the streets, and if you punk out one time, the rest of the hood rats would have you for lunch, you can believe that.

College was as boring as high school, but it didn't lack drama. In high school, the girls were just starting to grow their gardens and were all flirt and no action. Boys got their kicks from hiding under steps and checking out their Victoria's Secrets . Once in college, girls started to allow a bit more loitering in their playgrounds.

Faye, a marble-complexioned heartbreaker who would stroll the campus as if she had her name on the mortgage, could cause a stir just by walking into a room. She had a medium-built shapely frame with breasts so firm that they caused you to lose control of your saliva glands. You couldn't help but focus on her cleavage, which seemed to suck your eyes right out of their sockets. Her wardrobe consisted of nothing but mini dresses that hugged that ass like white on rice and stiletto heels that accented her shapely frame and killer legs to a point of making a brother lose his rocks from just looking at them. Her selection of outfits did not leave much to the imagination, and my imagination blew up when she was within smelling distance. Even the male teachers would crash their old asses into something looking at that man-eating mamma-jamma.

This girl was indeed fine and flirtatious, and she realized the animal magnetism that she created just by her sexy walk. She could have any dude on campus, including me, but she had chosen Shawn because he could knock a hole in a steel plate and, to cap it off, the sucker spent a fortune on her ass. She liked seeing him jealous to the point of leaving bodies scattered all over campus for just simply looking at her fine ass, and usually she got what she wanted. Faye had her white play toy, but there was no way Shawn could satisfy Faye. Hell, I don't know if anyone could, but here is one brother that would die trying to tame that Tasmanian she-devil. She scoped on me checking her out more than once but never played her hand. Fay made you commit because she had it like that. I had a dilemma because Faye was more of a challenge for my ego but Reba was the ultimate prize.

CHAPTER V

The Beatdown

It was Thursday and a school day, and I had to get to class on time. I woke to the smell of coffee, ham, eggs, and homemade biscuits coming from the kitchen. "Yo . . . Moms, someone is doing some serious burning up in here. Did Aunt Doll come over or something? 'Cause I know you ain't burning like that."

A voice came from the kitchen. "The word is *isn't*, AJ, not ain't. You are in college, so act like it."

"Well, Moms, since you put it like that . . . Isn't that grub slamming up in here?"

"AJ, you are just wasting your time down at that college talking like that. That thug attitude plays right into the hands of those who want you to fail."

"Ah, Moms, please just chill. I was just pulling your leg. I know how to use the queen's language when I need to. That's what gives us the edge, Moms, don't you know that?"

"It's king's English, not language. Your vocabulary is stuck on stupid, AJ."

"Moms, we can adjust to whatever we need in order to survive."

"Yeah, I remember at registration just how much of an edge you had with . . . What was her name? . . . Ah, ah. Tanya. Have you seen her or spoken with her?"

"Yeah, we are cool. I see her around campus."

"August James, what happened to that confidence that you had with her at registration? She must have burst that male ego bubble of yours, didn't she?"

"Mama, please, I don't want to talk about Tanya. Why you bring her up anyway?"

"Ouch . . . I struck a nerve, ex-squeeze me, Mr. Cool." Sometimes Moms could get on your last nerve, and she knows how to stick your ass and twist the knife. She is my Moms, but she was being a pain up in here.

As I entered the kitchen still groggy and wiping the sleep from my eyes, Aunt Doll grabbed me in one of her patented bear hugs. She was a huge woman who had a heart as big as she was. "Aunt Doll, I knew it must have been you," I said while trying to catch my breath from being swallowed up in her jumbo-sized tits. Things smelled too good, and I knew Moms couldn't warm a roll in the microwave without burning it.

"AJ, are you still as afraid of the dark as you were when you were little?" said Aunt Doll.

"Aunt Doll, just chill, you and Mama go around other folks talking that stuff. A brother has a reputation to uphold and that kind of talk can drop a dime on a brother."

Say what you want, but Aunt Doll could cook some grub and would be often heard fussing with mama about not giving Chantal a balanced meal before going to school. She would tell Mama that children need to learn on a full stomach. Her peach cobbler, mac and cheese, collard greens, and crackling cornbread taste so good it will make you slap your mama.

Now I know why when I go to the South to visit family and see all of the huge women, it's because they all eat like that down there. If you don't go back for seconds, it's an insult to them. If you have a somewhat thin frame like mine, they would say that you looked sickly. I don't know how healthy the food was, being cooked in all that grease and all, but it was the best I have ever had. The fried chicken, collard greens, mac and cheese, cornbread, fresh corn from the field, and some of the best lemonade you ever tasted will make your mouth water just smelling it.

I was twenty-one years old and still living at home with the parents for now, but it was a complete drag and I will be in the process of getting my own place when my money was right. This college thing was cramping my style, and I needed to make some money. I was in my sophomore year by now, and college had been a long haul for me. Though my family was cool, I had to have my space, and I couldn't do that without some serious money and my own crib. Basketball was my saving grace, but I struggled in the off-season. Occasionally, I would go to Hyde Park for a pickup game, but I had to make sure that it was somewhere out of the reach of Coach Boyd because he didn't believe in his players engaging in what he called street ball. When you play in the hood, you have to bring it or get embarrassed.

Moms was tall and stylish and had a walk that definitely exposed her credentials. Her brown eyes, soft voice, and big shapely legs drove Daddy crazy. He would always pretend that he was not the jealous type, but he always kept one eye on the world and the other on moms. Moms worked downtown at Mable's Beauty and Nail Salon. Every woman in town who loved the pampering scene always found her way to Mable's. All of the world's problems were solved at the beauty salons or the barber shops in the black communities. No matter how hard the work week had been, things were made all right when you got to the beauty salon or barber shop. You may not have been able to solve the world's problems, but it helped to talk about them, and there was always someone who was an expert at any subject that would come up. Most of these folks had not done well in life but could stroke their egos at the barber shop.

Pops had a decent gig as a restaurant inspector for the city of Chicago. He made sure that his work took him past the salon at least a couple times a day. I never understood why he was so insecure, because Moms worshipped that dude and wouldn't tip with anyone for all the tea in China. Pops came home on time and brought his check with him. He never stayed out late with the boys because he had something to come home to. I was one to talk when Reba had inundated my mind constantly for the last month, and I sure didn't want another dude tasting her cookies before I had a bite.

My Pops and I had what you would call a close relationship. He was too busy making ends meet and keeping a good eye on moms to give a shit about me. He never asked about school, never cared about how late I stayed out. I can't recall ever going to the park to throw the ball around or even go out in the empty lot to shoot baskets. The bonding thing was just out of the question. I felt like I was on my own anyway, so I looked forward to the day that I could move out of their way. I had no doubt that moms loved me, but her drinking had gotten to a point of no return and Daddy was too weak-minded to do anything about it. Mom was one of those drinkers who could still perform even when she was soused. Nothing prevented her from getting to the salon because that was where she got all of the juicy gossip about all the movers and shakers and the wannabes in the community.

My little sister Chantal was in the house, so I had to mind my behavior because she was my main concern. If she was harmed in any way by their lifestyle, I would never forgive them or myself. I wanted to get us both out of that apartment if I could. She was the prettiest little thing this side of creation. She was thirteen years old by now, had long brown pigtails, tall for her age, with beautiful cat eyes and skin so perfect and smooth that it felt like a baby's behind. Chantal had started to wear on me because she had started to blossom in all the right places, and I knew sooner or later I was going to have to lay one of those hardheads out for trying to touch her up. She reminded me so much of Reba because she was all about reading, study, and surfing the net on her laptop. If I needed any information for a report or parts for my car, she could find it on the internet. For a college dude, I was computer illiterate. Little piss-ant boys who think that she would be another notch on their belts better have another think coming. I knew that I couldn't watch her forever, but before forever came, they would have to come through me to get to her.

The night before, I could not get Reba out of my head. This girl had my mind all tied up in knots, and that made me a bit uneasy. I had never before thought twice about any pair of fine legs, so what made this set different? I had showered, put on one of my bitch-catching shirts, a pair of designer jeans, my Jordan sneakers, and topped it off with my brand-new black Chicago White Sox cap. My flowing curly locks protruding from under the cap made me look like Ice Cube. I was determined that day to impress Reba or die trying. I know she had noticed me but had too much uppity shit in her to recognize what a catch I could be. There were opportunities to converse with her on my co-op assignments in the newsroom, but my dumb ass blew every chance with some dumb and stupid macho remark that didn't hit the mark with Reba at all.

Though I had my reliable old 2010 Mustang parked in the garage, I preferred walking to school to save gas. It was a very fly ride but I needed a gas truck behind me cause that sucker drink petro like a fish needs water. I headed down Rose Avenue toward 53rd Street, looking down at my every step to keep from scuffing my new Jordan kicks. As I reached campus and headed for my 8:00 a.m. class in macro-economics, a voice came from the direction of Anderson Hall. "AJ, what's up? You're looking good enough to eat today, my nubian brother. Who are you trying to impress? Me, I hope." Glancing to the left of the entry to the building, I saw that it was a shapely female standing in the shade of the doorway.

No, it couldn't be, I thought to myself. After all, Faye had never given me the time of day. "Come here," the voice called out. "Come closer so I can lay my eyes on your fine self." Finally, I was close enough to see that it was Faye.

"What's up, Fabulous Faye, are you finally giving a brother some play?" Proceeding cautiously toward the opening where Faye was standing, I perused the surrounding area, hoping that Shawn the Mauler was nowhere in sight. "Girl, where is your white knight, Shawn?"

Faye mused, "What Shawn don't know surely won't hurt him and what I do is what I do because my destiny and your destiny is ours alone young stud and don't ever get it twisted. I have been waiting to holler at you for some time now" was her response.

"Girl, you are going to get both of us killed 'cause that crazy white caveman of yours loses his frickin' mind when a brother get anywhere near your fine ass."

"AJ, I never took you for a punk. Come over here and give a girl one of those big hugs 'cause you kicking it today, my brother. I just want an innocent hug from you, that's all, D-a-m-n. Why you trippin? Are you afraid that your little woman Ashley will chap your young ass? Come on over here to Faye and get this hug that's waiting for you." Now what the hell did she know about Ashley? Ash, is a good woman and I definitely don't want to drag her into any of my shit. Our relationship had been behind the scene so was a surprise to me that Faye was so pointed in her comment about Ash.

Something told me to acknowledge her and keep pushing because I was late anyway. My ego wouldn't let me pass up a once-in-a-lifetime chance to wrap my arms around a slice of Faye's heavenly pie.

As I reached to caress Faye and squeeze those melons of hers, she quickly placed her arms around my neck and pulled me so close to her that I could take her blood pressure. I could feel that strong heartbeat . . . or was it mine? Before I knew it, she was sucking my face in a way that had me reminiscing about being on a warm beach, sipping coconut rum in the Bahamas. I loved locking lips with that filly because she was no amateur, but I had to keep an eye out for Shawn. That white boy was hooked on that fine black meat. There is something to the old saying that if you ever go black, you will never go back, and Shawn's ass was bitten by that black widow spider.

As I responded to her aggression, her tongue darted to the back of my mouth, almost taking the little breath that I had left. By this time, my tool was so hard it almost pierced the silk mini dress that hugged Faye's body like warm, soft icing on one of Aunt Doll's prize-winning German chocolate cakes. Faye, feeling the effects of her body on my throbbing tool, smiled sensuously and asked, "Did I do that?" Just as I was about to answer, out of the study hall walked Reba, who strutted past us as if she wasn't even aware that we existed. Damn, of all the times for her to walk her fine ass by here. Did she actually see us, or was she so focused and in her own world as she usually was? I was hoping that she was as focused as usual and didn't pay attention to what and who was around her as she usually does. I didn't want to blow a chance to be with Reba, even for someone like Faye.

At that moment, Vickie, one of Faye's friends, approached and warned Faye that Shawn was heading in the direction of the study hall. "AJ, you better leave now, but we will finish this later, if you can handle it," said Faye. As I was still trying to clear my head from Faye sucking every ounce of breath out of me and the near miss with Reba, I moved slowly toward Cameron Hall where my economic class was being held. I had completely lost track of time and was within five minutes of being late for old man Stinson's class. Realizing that Professor Stinson was no joke and hated tardiness, I picked up the pace to a slight jog. As I rounded the corner headed for the steps leading to my class, I bumped into, of all people, Shawn. "What's up, AJ? In a hurry?"

"Yeah, man, just a bit late for class."

"Cool, catch you later then." Shawn and I were always casual with each other and indirectly realized that there was some type of competition going, but it had never been a problem. We were in different sports and tended to run in different circles. He had no reason to suspect me of anything . . . until now.

Shawn, looking back at me as I did at him while scurrying away, headed in the direction of the study hall where Faye usually hung out between classes. As he approached the hall, he passed Keisha, one of Faye's posse members. Shawn muttered, "Hey, Keisha, have you seen Faye around? I was trying to catch up with her before my next class." I should have my head examined to leave Keisha alone in a conversation with Shawn. That girl's mouth has leaks all around and if Shawn asked, she would definitely tell him about my and Faye's impromptu meeting.

Just as I found out later, Keisha did exactly what I had feared. With the energy of a Canary, Keisha started to sing, "Yeah, the last time I saw her, she was talking with AJ, and quiet as it's kept, you better watch that dude. He got his eyes on your prize, if you ask me. He was standing mighty close, and the two was looking quite chummy to me if you know what I mean. See you later, Shawn." Shawn turned in the direction that he had last seen me as if to say "Why didn't that punk mention that he had been talking with my woman?" When Shawn reached the study hall, Faye was nowhere to be found.

Shawn, known for losing it when Faye was in the mix, skipped the rest of his classes and parked himself at the entry to the campus, knowing that both Faye and I would have to pass him headed home. All students would normally use the front exit to leave campus because the strip outside of campus had all of the burger joints and happy hour bars. After several hours of waiting on those cement benches, Shawn had worked himself up and was now pacing back and forth. It had to be a hundred degrees in that quadrangle with all of the cement, and Shawn had gotten himself so worked up that sweat had completely soaked his muscle shirt that was so tight that he was about to burst out of it. The dude's muscles had muscles. In the state of mind that he was in, I don't think the heat mattered. "Man, where is that son of a bitch," said Shawn? "I will cancel his Christmas," he screamed in a loud threatening voice.

It was 4:00 p.m. and most classes were over by 3:30, and Shawn knew that it was only a matter of time before the crowd would pour out into the quadrangle. At a distance, Shawn could see Faye and her posse coming toward the entry as they would normally do about that time. Keisha had failed to tell Faye of her conversation with Shawn and would regret the oversight. Faye, seeing Shawn, blurted out, "What's up, baby? Were you waiting on your better half?" Faye could see that Shawn was in one of those foul moods as he would normally get when she had pissed him off. "What's up, boo?" she said. "What's wrong?"

"I should be asking you what's up, Faye. I heard that you been getting chummy with that dude AJ who you know I don't want around you 'cause he thinks he is big shit anyway. AJ and I are cool, but not when it comes to my girl, so what's up?"

"Nothing's up, and that was a few days ago when I was talking to AJ on the way to class," said Faye.

"Why you lying, Faye? Keisha told me that you and AJ was talking a few hours ago. And since you are lying, there must be something to what Keisha said. You better tell me something before I go off on somebody"

If looks could kill, Keisha would be a dead-ass posse member. Looking at Keisha, Faye said, "Keisha said what!"

Keisha, knowing that payback from Faye would be hell, dropped her head and slowly slid in behind Freddy, another posse member. Keisha knew that a mistake like she had just made could cause her exit from the posse permanently. Those who had crossed Faye in the past had to leave the area or suffer the consequences, from being ostracized to being discovered in some alley, a victim of some unknown beat-down.

Though Faye was undoubtedly the queen of fine, she was also from the streets and was well-connected with the sleaze factors and knew how to get things done without it tracking back to her. At that moment, I was approaching the group, unaware that Shawn had found out about my short escapade with Faye.

Shawn turn to see me coming, hurriedly walked toward me and without saying a word, coldcocked me with a roundhouse punch that Sugar Ray Leonard would have been proud of. "What the hell Shawn, why you trippin," I said. To make matters worse, as I tumbled backward from the punch to the right side of my face, I just happened to have landed at the feet of who else but Reba, who again was just passing through the quadrangle on her way to the newspaper room. Now I knew what being in hell was like. On one hand, I had a big mouth full of Shawn's knuckle sandwich, and on the other, I was embarrassed in front of Reba, whom I so terribly wanted to impress. I could see my vision of ever being with her going up in smoke. The game plan that I had crafted had just gone up in smoke. "Shawn, I'll give you that one but pay back is hell, old AJ can take one licking and keep on ticking."

Out of the corner of my now blackened and swollen eye, I could see Faye leaving with Shawn, still trying to convince him that nothing happened between her and me. As they moved away, Faye glanced over her shoulder and gave me a wink just to say "I got power, and I can do whatever the hell I want and get away with it."

Keisha, knowing that she had crossed the line with Faye, came over to me to apologize. "AJ, my bad, I had planned to tell Faye about seeing Shawn, but I forgot."

"What did you tell that crazy dude anyway, Keisha? You know how insane he gets at just the mention of Faye's name?"

"I just told him that the last time I saw Faye, she was talking to you, that's all."

"Girl, that was enough to set that fool off, and now I will have to face him again because I am not going to take this beat-down without a payback. That's the rules, and even he knows it. Punking out is not an option, Keisha, you know that. Apologizing to me is the least of your problems. You need to figure out how to deal with Faye. I have heard stories about what has happened to those who have crossed that crazy woman in the past. You better watch your donkey girl."

"I know, and whatever happened, AJ, I just want you to know how sorry I am. Maybe I can make it up to you somehow. I mean, you know . . . in any way you want me to . . . any way."

Can you believe this shit? I said to myself. *Here I am, lying on my ass and nursing a fat black eye, and this girl is trying to ride my joystick.* Though Keisha ain't hard on the eyes, popping that was not high on my priority list. "Look, Keisha, you had better figure out how to deal with that crazy-ass Faye. You know she is not going to let this go. You and I will settle up later."

"Thanks for not being too upset with me, AJ, I owe you big time."

This was not the last that Faye and Shawn would hear from me, you can believe that.

I lay there on the grass for what seemed like an hour, partly embarrassed and mostly feeling stupid for allowing Faye to make me one of Shawn's punching bags. As I pulled myself together, I realized that it was my evening to work in the newspaper room with Reba. My day had gone from worse to disastrous. How do I face her with a swollen jaw, black eye, and bruised ego? I could just go home and not help Reba, but that's the coward's way out. I had gotten myself into this mess, so not going to help Reba was not an option. AJ, suck it up and face the music, I said to myself. You got yourself into this mess, so man up.

When I entered the newsroom, Reba was sitting at the desk, using the computer to do the layouts for the next edition of the school paper. She briefly looked up at me and said, "Oh, hi, AJ. I didn't hear you come in. There is a ton of things to get done today before the next issue comes out. I thought you were not coming, seeing that you had a pretty busy day. I have to say you looked quite comfortable lying face down in the grass." I wouldn't have been that concerned about it had she not been smiling as if she was enjoying the moment. She acted as if she didn't notice all the damage to my mug.

The phone rang in the back office, and Reba excused herself to answer it. After a few minutes of whispering it seemed, she came back into the layout room. "AJ, that was my father that called, and he is coming to campus. Would you mind walking with me, and I can introduce you to him?"

"You bet your ass I would, Reba."

"AJ, why is it necessary for you to have such a foul mouth? You know I don't appreciate that mess."

"OK, my bad, Reba. I would love to meet your father."

"Now, doesn't that sound a lot better," she said with a smile? "He will be here in a few minutes. I had asked if he would drop one of my books off that I left in his car earlier this week. I think you will enjoy meeting him, I hope so any way." That's the most positive thing Reba has said to me in a while.

We waited a few minutes and started to walk toward the main entrance to the campus where we were to meet Reba's father.

Naturally, I was curious about her parents because she had such a sultry and exotic look that there had to be some cross-pollination going on. Her roots were from the big house, not from the slave quarters. Old massa and Aunt Sarah met in the wee, wee hours of the morning to start the process that eventually ended up producing this fine specimen of a woman. You know the massa had to have some of that dark meat every once in a while.

As we approached the entrance, there was a curly-haired, young-looking white guy standing next to the flagpole. He was tall (approximately six feet two, I would guess), lean, and had that look of authority about him. As we got closer to the entrance, it seemed that he was smiling at us. No, this couldn't . . . Before I could say another word, Reba rushed to meet him with a hug and kiss. "Thanks, Daddy, for bringing my book. It was a relief knowing that it was in your car. I thought that I had left it in one of my classes. Daddy, I want you to meet a friend who works in the newsroom with me. AJ, this is my father, Dr. James Eckersley. Daddy . . . this is AJ."

"How are you, AJ? Any friend of my little girl is a friend of mine."

I am losing my edge. It should have dawned on me that her father was white because when have you ever known a brother named Eckersley? I was so busy checking out the finer things in life and didn't even think about her last name. Now I am really wondering because her mom must be one fine black queen to have constructed the likes of Reba.

Man, this guy must have had his clothes specially cut for him because, I have to say, he was definitely representing. He had on a blue-striped Armani suit, accented with a blinding white shirt, gold silk tie, pocket to match and a pair of diamond cuff links to match the tie stick pin. I couldn't help but glance down at his feet because the shoes usually places the look in perspective. If the shoes are not slamming, the rest of the package doesn't follow. It's like having a clean car with dirty tires or a thousand-dollar suit with sneakers. He had on some black Italian gators shined to the max on top of some cold silk socks. I also noticed the diamond-studded Rolex watch, which sparkled like new money. His shirt collar and cuff had the initials DJE on them.

All of my suspicions about Reba were true. I knew she must have been a zebra. He was so prim and proper that he made me nervous, and the dude had a grip like a vice for a slim dude. "Pleased to meet you, sir," I said, feeling a little out of place and thinking now that I really was out of this girl's league.

"So, AJ, what are you majoring in?"

I wanted to say "Your daughter," but instead I said, "Business admin, sir."

"That's great, AJ. Lord knows we need more good businessmen, if you know what I mean. Have you thought about which grad school you want to attend after undergrad?"

I should have guessed that a dude like him would start Truth or Consequences. Why is he asking all of these questions, I said to myself, and not once has he asked about the shiner that I had? "No, sir, not yet, but I will decide soon."

"Well, that's good, AJ. Maybe we can talk more about this later because I have to run to a conference across town."

As we shook hands and he kissed Reba good-bye, the one thing I was not looking forward to was another question-and-answer session with the doctor. It was as if he could look right into my soul. As he approached the curb where a black town car was waiting, he quickly turned and, in a very forceful voice, said, "Reba and AJ . . . I am having a small dinner gathering on Saturday. Why don't you kids drop by? It will give me an opportunity to continue our conversation, AJ. See you there." Before we could respond, he had disappeared into the backseat of the limo. That had to be the longest fifteen-minute conversation I had ever had. You would have thought that I had just asked for Reba's hand in marriage the way he was smoking me over.

I had no intentions of going to the dinner party until Reba brought it up again. "AJ, it would be nice if we could go by for a little while . . . Please? It would make Daddy so happy."

"Reba, I would love to, but not this Saturday."

"Oh, come on, AJ, you are just trying to make up some excuse. I am counting on your going so that we don't disappoint daddy. So what do you say?"

"Let me think about it, Reba. You know, all of this is so sudden, and a man has to have a little air. Your dad was pressing hard, and I don't want to have to play twenty questions when I get there. I will let you know tomorrow."

I could see that Reba was disappointed in my hesitance to go to her parents' home for dinner, but her father made me uncomfortable, and I didn't really know why. I definitely was not because her father was white, because I suspected something was different about her from the start. Maybe it was because I was not sure where my college career was going, and I didn't want to be pressed on the subject by her father. To accept the invitation would be stepping off into a world that I knew was deep water for me, and I am not a great swimmer.

A slight mist of rain had started to blanket the area, and I took the opportunity to pull Reba closer to me and cover her head with my light jacket. I don't know why, but when things were overcasted like they were, it put me in a solemn mood. I could tell that Reba was appreciative of the gesture. "Thanks, AJ. I really didn't want to get my hair wet. You know a girl has to keep her hair slamming." Slamming, I said to myself. Is this the same Reba? She never uses slang. For the next few blocks of our walk back, things were quiet between us. As we got closer to the newsroom, I couldn't help but ask, "Reba, what kind of a doctor is your father? He seems very nice."

"He is a cardiologist, and he is currently working on ways of eliminating the condition called enlarged heart syndrome."

With every step, I felt smaller and smaller in terms of dealing with Reba. Maybe I should stay with someone like Ashley. With her, I never had to be on the defensive as much as when I was with Reba. I felt that I was the authority with Ash, but with Reba I felt that I should be sitting in a corner with a dunce cap on.

"AJ, you seem to be in deep thought. What's up? If you are trippin' about going to my parent's home, then don't do it."

"Oh no, it's not that, Reba. Just thinking how impressive your father is. I can see a lot of him in you. He is self-assured, confident of his position in life, comfortable in his own skin and a picture of accomplishment."

"AJ, what a nice thing for you to say! That was sweet. You try so hard to impress with that macho attitude, but deep down inside, you are a teddy bear."

"Well, bears get a big hug, so hug me, Reba."

"AJ, you got all of the hugs you are going to get on the walk back, my brother."

I knew that I had no intention of ever having dinner with her father and be grilled about my future. As we entered the newsroom, Reba seemed in a great mood but had still not mentioned the beat down. I really wanted to taste that nectar, but this brother was going to distance himself from this prime real estate. Today's events made me more convinced of that than ever. I had to figure out a way to get out of going to dinner without hurting her feelings.

As the evening wore on, her behavior was getting the best of me, so I had to approach her about what had happened in the quadrangle. "Reba, speaking of what happened earlier today between Shawn and me, I am so sorry that you had to see my beat down. That dude coldcocked me when I wasn't looking. He surprised me and did not give me a chance to defend myself."

"AJ, whatever happened between you and Shawn is between the two of you . . . and Faye, and doesn't involve me." She mentioned Faye in a very suggestive way of letting me know that she was paying more attention than maybe I had given her credit for. There was even a little movement of the neck as most black sisters will do when they are upset. Now I am wondering just how much she really saw between Faye and me this afternoon.

"What do you mean, Reba, what's Faye gotta do with this?"

Reba snapped her head around as if to say, "AJ, please." Her look made it obvious that she did see me sucking face with Faye. She must have, or she wouldn't have said that. "AJ, what you do is your business, but as quiet as it's kept, you got what you deserved. You knew already how jealous Shawn is about that floozy Faye, but you were messing with her anyway," said Reba, obviously steamed by the conversation. She had responded as if it had struck a nerve. The easygoing girl that I had just walked back with had become a neck-moving, psychological, flame-spurting adversary. Actually it was turning me on because that was her black side coming out, and man, did I love it. *Get your loins back in your britches, AJ,* I said to myself. But I couldn't back away from this fine girl who could get me to give up my player's card any day of the week by just asking. I wouldn't be myself if I didn't carry this a bit further because quitting now would always leave a question in my mind about what could have been. But there was still the question about going to dinner.

Reba seemed really upset when I brought up Faye. Was this an opening? Does she really care a little and just didn't want to admit it? Was that icy shell finally starting to crack? As we finished the evening, I did see a slight glance in my direction and just a hint of a smile. Maybe there was hope after all. Maybe if she did see what happened between Faye and me, it was somewhat of a turn-on, and old AJ just might be back in business.

I managed to slide right out of the dinner invitation by not seeing Reba or answering her calls until the following week. Even after I had flaked out on her the Saturday before, Reba seemed a bit friendlier toward me, and we shared more of our personal situations with each other. I was careful not to screw it up this time, so I took it slow and easy. Though she had on several occasions asked me to dinner with her folks, I would always have a conflict. I couldn't continue to refuse if I was to ever have a chance with her.

CHAPTER VI

Beatdown Redemption

Now that I had started to get a foothold in a possible relationship with Reba, I couldn't help but think about the beat down that Shawn had laid on me and the smirk on Faye's face as they left me sprawled on the Northwestern seal etched in the cement in the quadrangle. There had to be a way to get back at Faye without another confrontation with Shawn. Not only was Faye Shawn's girl, but that dude spent crazy money on her ass all the time. Who wouldn't get a little smoked if some other dude was wading in her sexy pond? She had stepped out of line once before with a guy from Carver High School, and Shawn had not only attempted to rearrange her beautiful face but gave the guy such a beating that he had to leave school. It was the one and only time that he had laid his hands on her but it could be the opening that I needed. This lady was not one you put your hands on in a violent way more than once.

No matter how flirtatious Faye was, she did not want to cross the line and risk the wrath of Shawn again. Shawn also knew that Faye was not the type that would allow herself to be slapped around.

I knew that she would often get her hair done on Thursdays around 5:00 p.m. at the shop where Moms worked. During that time, Shawn was usually working at Macy's department store, on the loading docks, after class. The dude was a hustler and was making decent scratch, enough to keep Faye happy and I knew she didn't want to give up the meal ticket. His shift didn't end until after 10:00 p.m., which would give me plenty time to work the magic on Faye. Faye was good, but old AJ was a little better. I came from the same streets that she did, so it was now my time to turn the tables.

It was Thursday evening of the following week, and payback time. I drove my red 2010 Mustang convertible toward downtown, passing the University of Chicago Booth School on North City, front Plaza Drive, and down along the Chicago River, and parked a few streets over from the salon to wait for Faye to come out from her hair and nail appointment. After about a couple of hours in the chair, touching up her hair and getting it fried, dyed, and laid to the side, Faye strolled out wearing a short leopard dress, some pumps that stretched her frame another five inches, and bling that sparkled with every sexy step. I allowed her to get several blocks from the shop so that I was not seen by my moms, who could blow my plans if she saw me. I also have to admit it was quite exciting following behind that fine piece of flesh, with her hips giving you a sexual experience with every step taken.

I followed at a distance for a while just to take in the motion of that backside ocean. The girl had it all and then some. I pulled up beside her and, with excitement in my voice said, "Ms. Faye, with your fine self, it's AJ. What's up, girl?"

"AJ, you aren't still mad at me, are you? You know a girl got to do what a girl got to do."

"No doubt, Faye, but where are you headed now?"

"Oh, just to do some more shopping before I go home. What's in that devious mind of yours? I can see from the look and smirk on your handsome face, that you are scheming something so talk to me."

"Girl, get in the car. I know a little burger joint on the river that is very secluded, and you owe me that for that beat down anyway. You remember you promised to take up where we left off, unless you didn't mean it. Or are you punking out like you told me?"

"AJ, I don't want any more trouble with Shawn, and you shouldn't either."

"Girl, like you told me, what Shawn don't know won't hurt him. I have as much to lose as you do. If Ashley sees your fine self getting into my ride, my ass is grass and she would be a lawnmower. So get in, girl. I will get you home before the dude gets off his gig, I promise."

Knowing that Faye has always lived on the edge, I knew she couldn't resist, and quite honestly, I do believe there was chemistry between us if only sexual. "Okay AJ, I ain't playing with you, you better get me home before Shawn comes by my apartment. By the way, I took care of Keisha's ass for ratting us out. That whore did that on purpose because she has always had a thing for Shawn. Her trifling ass thought I didn't know what a backstabbing bitch she was. What Ican say is that her ass won't rat on me ever again, you can believe that."

"Faye, what the hell did you do to that girl?"

"AJ, quit asking questions and drive. What happened to Keisha is between her and me. Did you have a thing for Keisha, AJ? I hope the hell not or you can let me out of this car right now."

"Chill, Faye . . . Damn . . . And quit raising your voice. I could have had Keisha anytime I wanted, but why swim with minnows when you can ride around with the big fish?"

"Now you talking my type shit, AJ. I didn't hurt the bitch, just left her understanding what time it really is. She had to know that I would eventually find out."

As I put a little pep in my step, the phone started to ring. Now who can this be? As I checked the screen on my phone, I could see it was Reba, but how could I talk to her with Faye all up in my mug? So I decided to let it ring which prompted her to say, "damn AJ, that ringing is getting on my nerves. Why don't you answer that thing? Or is it one of your ladies checking on you?"

"Quit trippin', Faye, I got this.

"Hello."

"Hello, AJ, what are you up to? I just thought maybe we can hang out before I have to go to the library."

"Oh, that is a nice suggestion, but I can't right now. AJ Looking over at Faye said, "I have a lot of stuff to do before night fall so I will call you back later. OK, good-bye."

As I glanced over at Faye, she had this smirk on her face and was not buying the vanilla discussion that I just had. "AJ, you are a trip. That was obviously one of your play toys so who was she?"

"That was just a friend of mine, Faye, so what's the big deal?"

"You are straight-out lying and the truth ain't in you. You could have talked to whoever she is, I'm cool. It must have been your little nookie, Ashley, checking on your young ass, or was it that Reba chick that you almost fainted over her seeing us sucking face that day at the library? AJ, just handle your business," said Faye with a deeper and sarcastic tone.

"Man, I get tired of these bitches reading me like some used book," AJ mumbled to himself. "The luster is definitely leaving the game, and I can't afford to have that happen. Since when has the hunter been captured by the game?"

My timing was wack, and I again had given up another opportunity to hang out with Reba. I was slowly coming to the realization that Reba and I weren't on the same wave cycle. Every time she had made the effort to spend time with me, I had my head in the proverbial sand, like now. I was in this thing to win it, so there was absolutely no way I was going to let Faye out of my grasp. This thing between Faye and I would come to a head one way or another. And this was a prime opportunity.

As we drove toward the river and Lake Shore Drive, I couldn't help glancing over at her legs, which were very visible, and the leopard dress, which was so short that I could almost see her sunshine. "AJ, you must see something you want." Faye was quite aware of what I was doing as she played along by moving her hips side to side with the beat of Barry White's song, *Practice What You Preach*", which was totally appropriate. It goes like this:

Girl, there is something wrong with me
'cause every time I'm alone with you,
you keep talking about you loving me.
Hey babe, your foreplay just blows my mind,
so why don't we stop all this talking girl,
why don't we stop wasting time?

I've had my share of lovers,
some say I'm damn good,
and if you think you can turn me out,
baby I wish that you would,
'cause you keep telling me this, and telling me that,
and once I am with you I can never go back.

"Ms Faye, All I can tell you tell you, is you may have to practice what you preach girl."

"Barry said it better than I could, Faye. I tell you, baby girl, if you ever get a piece of old AJ, you will throw rocks at Shawn, and you can believe that. I do practice what I preach, and you better believe that."

Faye just smiled and kept moving to the music, getting me all greased up. "Boy, if you had some of this, you wouldn't live to tell about it," she shot back. "I ain't found a sucker yet who can really handle this, including Shawn. Shawn is just a means to an end, if you know what I mean. He is well-connected and can get a girl what she needs. He is all right, but he can't feed my moJo baby boy, and I doubt if you can either." "Man, this hamma was trippin and really knows how to challenge a brotha". I would give that thing a black eye, put a seven-inch gash in her cerebellum, and definitely make that liver quiver, and you can believe that.

Barry's words just served to fire me up more and increase my expectations. It was time for her to put up or shut up. Faye had talked a good game, so now it's time to get on the scoreboard. We arrived at the burger joint and spent the next hour taking in the scenery. The restaurant was strategically placed overlooking the most scenic part of the lake. It was the perfect setting to test my assumption about Faye, that of seeing if she was as interested in testing me sexually as I was in testing her. We had two pitchers of beer and some of those little fish-looking cheese crackers and peanuts, and I could see that Faye was getting a slight buzz. I didn't have much money in my pocket, so I was hoping that she would fill herself with the crackers and beer and not want to order anything else. Faye had a big appetite and that big girl could throw down some grub but she seemed happy munching on the crackers and sucking down the beer.

I was sitting directly across from Faye when all of a sudden I could feel her foot slowly rubbing the inside of my leg which was causing immediate hard feelings, if you know what I mean. I could see that it was turning her on as much as it was me. As she moved up my leg and was rubbing my tool with her foot, she was licking her inviting me to come along.

"All right girl, you are playing with fire now, you better believe that."

She shot back, "Either you got more fuel to fan these flames or you are going to pour water on it little man. This fire will burn your ass if you don't handle it carefully."

Now this big hammer is pushing my button and it's like the streets, a brother can't punk out now. She will be calling me big man after I knock the roof off that sucker. Shawn can't venture into the deep waters like old AJ and this beautiful piece of female is about to find out.

It was part of the plan to select this place because upstairs were rental rooms, which made my plan that much easier. I asked Faye to excuse me for a minute and that I would be back shortly.

I had already rented a room hoping that Faye wouldn't reject me and my invitation. As I approached the front desk, one of the white guys on the desk recognized me. "You are AJ and you play for Northwestern, don't you?"

"Yeah, man, you must have seen one of my games."

"Yeah, right," said the desk clerk. Man everyone around campus know that you can ball when you want too." This was a little strange that this dude recognized me. What I didn't know was that he was a friend of Shawn and his seeing me and Faye together would start another string of incidents with that Neanderthal. It was destined to happen anyway.

After checking to see if the room was ready, I returned to the patio where Faye was sitting and could see that the beer was kicking in and the girl was ready for just about anything. "AJ, where were you? You can't leave a sister sitting alone for such a long time. Some of the guys sitting over by that window over there would love to take your place," she said with a sexy, lip-licking smile.

"The best thing they can do is admire from a distance and go and whack off because there is nothing over here for them, and you can bet on that. Now come on, girl, I want to show you something." I reached for her hand and slowly pulled her toward me.

Faye said with a sheepish look on her face, "Are we leaving, AJ? I am not ready to go." With a smile and a wink, I was about to lead this fine-ass sheep to the slaughter. " Ms Faye, you are in good hands with AJ so come on with me girl."

I had a vision of that day when she and Shawn had walked away from me after the beat down, and now payback was going to be a bitch. As we strolled past the desk, Alex, the desk clerk who had spoken to me, was standing behind the door to the back office. What I didn't know was that he had seen Faye sitting on the patio and didn't want to be recognized because Faye would have identified him as a friend of Shawn. I was also to find out later that this little evening get-together would not be unknown to Shawn.

We arrived at room 119, which happens to be 9/11 backwards. Like 9/11, this was shaping up to be one of those situations that will remain with me for a long time and represent a life-changing experience. Faye blurted out, "I thought we were leaving AJ. You know if you go in to this room, you may not come out with that huge ego intact." This could be the beginning of a good thing or an ego deflating experience for me," murmured AJ under his breath.

Once inside the room, it was obvious that Faye had been a key participant in this script many times before. I had a dime bag of weed in my pocket and what a great way to set the mood. I had said that I was going to keep away from the weed for a while but I had to use every tool in my bag to get a saddle on this filly. "Hey, Faye, let's take a hit off of some of this good stuff and take in the scenery." The room had a view of the balcony that was no less than spectacular. I quickly lit a joint and took a long and satisfying drag, closed my eyes, and let the aroma tickle my nostrils. Faye, instead of taking her own drag, placed her lips over mine to share my portion. It surprised me but was more than welcome. The smell of her perfume, her soft wet lips, and the smell of the weed sent us both to another level. There was no doubt in my mind now what was about to happen.

The room was tastefully decorated with a double bed, a minibar, ceiling lights, and a large mirror which would come in handy as I moved deeper into the moment. His and hers robes was hanging by the door, which gave the room a little taste. In the bath area was a tub and a double showerhead that looked like something from outer space. The radio next to the bed was playing soft jazz and two mints lay on the lamp table to the right of the bed. The bedspread and curtains were a pale yellow, which accented the very appropriate wall paintings of scenes in Italy, and colorful rugs were arranged strategically throughout the room. To the right of the bed stood a stand and bucket with some cheap champagne and two glasses. Not bad for a boy from the projects, even though moms was paying for all of this. If she knew how I was using her money, I would be cut off for good. I may not have had much scratch in my pocket, but I knew how to impress. In order to get the best, you have to give the best.

"Look, Faye, let's sit here for a minute and continue to enjoy some of this good stuff." Each time I took a hit from the weed, she would place her lips on mine. Her lips were soft and tender and tasted sweet as if she had just consumed a bouquet of sweet roses. This woman was hot as a stick of dynamite and carried twice the explosive.

After taking a few more drags off the weed, Faye wasted no time in taking my hand and placing it on those fine melons, and pulled me into her web just as she had done on campus. After a moment of teasingly running her hand up the inseam of my trousers, she stood up and started to slowly unzip her dress. I sat on the edge of the bed, taking it all in. First, the dress dropped slowly to the floor, exposing a red bra that barely covered her nipples and a red G-string that was smoking from the fire between her legs. I started this as payback, but now I am wondering if I knew what the hell I was getting myself into. This woman was so fine it was scary. She had curves in places that most girls didn't have places. That body of hers was built for speed and endurance, and I was about to find out how fast and how long I could hang with this girl who had a body by Fisher and a mind by Mattel. My reputation was at stake, and I had to represent.

While she was doing her mating dance for me, I had quickly removed my trousers, getting ready for the main event. She asked me to lie back on the bed and let her take me to a place I had never been before, and I was more than happy to oblige. For the first time in my life, I had to admit that I was unsure of myself. What if I couldn't keep up with this man killer? What if she turns me out? How could I face anyone on campus if Faye dogs a brother out? She is the type that will tell on your ass if you can't step up to the plate. I was hoping that I had brought my "A" game because from the looks of what was standing in front of me, I would need an A plus. It was definite too late to back out now.

Her hands began to explore my chest, my stomach, and in one motion, her tongue started to caress my belly button in a circular motion while she was removing my shorts. This was a pro, and I was now in up to my proverbial neck. Was backing out before the fireworks start be in my best interest? With each circular motion of her tongue, she would start sucking my navel until my tool sprung up like a jack-in-the-box.

Things were moving so quickly that it could have ended this episode as swiftly as it had started. My entire body was shaking. I couldn't allow her to continue down this road because it would be over before I could even start. The volcano deep within me was starting to boil much too quickly. She finished pulling my shorts over my throbbing tool and went to work on it with more vigor than what she had done to my belly button. She seemed pleased and a bit shocked at the size of my tool but wasted no time in totally consuming it and sending me into a state where I actually thought that I was losing my frickin' mind. As her warm tongue caressed and enveloped my manhood, my legs and lower body seemed numb as I was slowly but surely losing control.

I removed her bra to expose two of the most beautiful twins a woman could have. Her nipples were firm and standing at attention, like two soldiers saluting the flag. She straddled me, pulling aside her G-string, preparing to guide my tool into her hot oven. I had to take control or this woman was going to cause a gusher before I was ready, so

I forced her over on her back and spread her legs so wide that she gave out a loud moan as I entered her from the back. She seemed shocked at my sudden aggressiveness. I do pride myself on my attributes, and she was about to get all of what old AJ could give. As I forced my tool in her hot enclave, she gripped the sheets so hard that she pulled them from under the mattress. I knew then that I was in the game.

I pumped her harder and harder until she pleaded for me to stop. There was no stopping me now because I wanted to give her some of the medicine that I'm sure she had dished out to many unfortunate brothers that couldn't tame this Brahma bull. As I thrust deeper and deeper into her wet rose garden, she gave out grunts that were so sensual that I couldn't help but cry out in ecstasy with her. I tried my best to hold out and extend the episode of the best sex I had ever had, until she regained control by started to shiver all over. She started to shake her body with such passion that we both tumbled to the floor, still locked in each other's embrace and still mixing our potions.

We both grunted and groaned so loud that anyone in the adjoining room must have heard us, but who cared at that point. Faye yelled out my name and moaned in a manner that let me know that I had her at the top of the mountain and she was about to take the leap. We both hit the climax ceiling at the same moment right there on the carpet. I rolled off and laid face up staring at the ceiling with my eyes looking like the red white and blue cylinders rotating outside of a barber shop. Faye just laid on her side staring at me as if to say, "What the hell was that?"

I had experienced some heavy love-making in my young life, but nothing had ever taken me to this level. We were both soaked with our body juices and laid exhausted after about thirty wonderful minutes of sexual combat. It was the first time that I could remember that Faye was totally silent. We laid there for what seemed like hours on the rug without saying a word, just staring at the ceiling. Faye had her head on my chest and her legs wrapped around mine in a manner of resignation. We both had to know that this was going to be a problem. You don't have sex at this level and make it a one-time deal, but I wasn't ready to tempt fate and chance facing Shawn again. However, I knew this wasn't over by any stretch of the imagination. There would be another time for me and Faye, and I looked forward to it. I didn't care anymore about getting back at her for the beat-down because she had more than lived up to her reputation. Old AJ had truly represented, and you can believe that. We laid there for what seemed like hours, though it was only for a few minutes, just enjoying the moment and smelling the aroma of our great lovemaking episode. There just has to be a sequel.

We glanced at the clock by the bed and both realized that it was only an hour before Shawn would be off work and headed to Faye's apartment as was his normal routine. We gazed deeply into each other's eyes and, without hesitation, were again locked in each other's embrace as hot and heavy as the first time. This time she straddled me in the sitting position and in one motion, had mounted me again with the force of a jackhammer. Her thrusts were so hard and sensual that it brought me to a climax instantly, and I gave out a holler that pierced the quietness of the room. I rolled her off just to catch my breath. By this time, another thirty minutes had passed, and it would take some time to get dressed and at least twenty-five to thirty minutes to drive to Faye's crib.

As we dressed to leave, Faye remained quiet and reserved, and I tried to rejuvenate her by reminding her of the time and our need to get back before Shawn gets off. It was 8:00 p.m., and Shawn would be getting off the clock in about thirty minutes. He would only have about a twenty-minute drive to Faye's place, giving us just enough time to freshen up a bit and head to her place. For the first time, Faye didn't seem that concerned about the time or about Shawn. It concerned me though because I could always cover my flanks during the day, but at night, it was a little shaky and sometimes unnerving.

As I pulled up to Faye's apartment building, she slowly moved her head and eyes toward me before she said, "Okay, AJ, what now? I really don't know what happened, but I need to see you again." I got out of the car without a response and went around to the passenger side to let her out. I returned to the driver's side and, with a slight grin, I left her with the same look that I had gotten at the beat-down that said "I got the power now, and I can do whatever the hell I want and get away with it." I had given Faye some of her own medicine, but why didn't I feel good about it? I believe that she had made as much an impact on me as I had on her. There would be a sequel to this day, you can bet on it.

I quickly hurried to get into my car and had started to pull away when a silver Lexus pulled in front of me, and out of the passenger seat stepped Alex, the clerk that had seen me at the hamburger joint. Had he seen Faye too? From the driver side stepped Shawn, dressed in tight jeans and a body shirt that displayed every ripple in his perfectly sculptured 220-pound body. I knew then that Shawn had gotten the down low on what had happened between Faye and me. Stepping out of the car with his hands above his head, Shawn stated, "AJ, here we are again, dude, and with my girl again."

Faye, knowing what Shawn was about to do, jumped between Shawn and me and began to explain that I had picked her up downtown and was bringing her home and that was all. Shawn, without thinking, slapped Faye with the back of his hand, knocking her to the ground. "Faye, you are a lying sack of shit, and I am tired of putting up with your crap. I don't need your ass anyway. I know you and this dude was knocking boots down by the river. My posse is all over, and your ass can't hide. I treat your ass like a queen, and this is my payback?"

Seeing Shawn slap Faye brought out the Rambo in me. Without even thinking, I bum rushed Shawn grabbing him by the shoulder and as he turned, I put all of my 185 pounds into a punch that sent him stumbling against the car. Knowing that he was only temporarily dazed, I quickly move to the backseat of my car to get a hickory stick that I kept for dogs. I was not about to take another embarrassing beat-down, and I was not going to allow him to whip up on Faye like that. As Shawn turned around preparing to retaliate, I stepped toward him with the stick and swung it so hard that it gave off a sound that startled him and his posse. The force of the swing stopped him cold in his tracks.

For the first time, Shawn ended up on the short end of my beat-down and I was confident that if he wanted some more of old AJ, it was there for the taking. Shawn looked at me and at Faye, who was still lying on the sidewalk dazed from the slap, pointed his finger at the both of us, and ran his finger across his throat as if to say we were dead meat, before jumping into his car and speeding away. I knew it wouldn't be the last I would hear from that dude, but the die had been cast.

"AJ, I am so sorry to have gotten you into this again. How did he know we were together anyway?"

"That punk, Alex, who was riding with him, I saw him at the hotel when we were there. You didn't see him when we passed the front desk, and I didn't know that he was Shawn's friend. Faye, you are too good a person to put up with that dude. Any chump who would hit a woman is a coward and don't deserve your company."

"You got that right, AJ, but it will be hard for me without Shawn's help. I can't afford this apartment on my own."

"Well, Faye, as I see it, you got a choice of either continuing to be his doormat or holding your head up and figuring it out on your own. Girl, you have a gift for design, just look at you. I will talk to my friend André and see if he can use your skill in his dress shop on 5th and High."

"Would you do that for me, AJ, after all of the problems that I have caused you?"

"Sweet lady, after the time that you and I had today, that is the least I can do."

I took my thumb and rubbed a slight tear away as I cupped her face in my hands. "You are indeed a special woman who deserves to be treated with dignity and respect. This was bound to happen between Shawn and me. It was just a matter of time. I just hate that you had to be in the middle of it."

"Thanks, AJ, that's the nicest thing that anyone has ever said to me. You make me feel special, not because of how I look or because of my figure, but because you see me, the person, and I appreciate that more than you know."

I gave her a slight kiss on one jaw and then the other and turned to leave when Faye grabbed my arm and asked, "What now, AJ? You have truly rocked my world in more ways than one, so what now?" With a wink and a smile, I left Faye pondering the answer. I knew it wouldn't be the last I would see of Faye, but I had to have my space for a while. Faye is like that potato chip commercial; you can't just have one and not want more. She had just made it that much harder for the other women in my life. There was not a chance that I would pass up another day like this with Faye, not a chance.

It was Friday now, and the last day of the semester and another opportunity to spend the evening with Reba in the newsroom as we approached the end of the semester. No matter the great time I had spent with Faye, I was determined to get a final breakthrough with Reba, and this was the day. Reba walked in wearing a pair of designer jeans that showed every curve on her well-sculptured body. Though not quite as sexy as Faye, she could turn heads by simply walking into a room. Down the side of the jeans was the word perfect, and written across the chest of her black, sequenced blouse, was the word Jesus Treasure. It was the first time that Reba had allowed this more tantalizing side of her to show. I was like ex-president Jimmy Carter; I was committing sin all over the place in my mind. Was Reba dressed like this to impress me? I would like to think so. After all, she showed the sensitive side the other day. Did she feel that she needed to dress a little more provocatively to be in the game? I hoped so.

As the evening wore on, I found myself daydreaming about the evening with Faye, but Reba had also noticed my preoccupation. "AJ, why are your eyes so red, and why do you seem preoccupied? What's up?"

"Oh, nothing, Reba, just a little tired today. I could use a little company after work. I just don't feel like going home right away. There is a little deli not too far from here, and I would be honored if you would share a sandwich and a cup of coffee with me."

"Wow, AJ, since you say it that way, how can I refuse? What's gotten into you, being so polite and all?"

"Okay, Reba, give a brother a break. You are so used to seeing the ghetto side of a brother that you have never noticed that I can be quite a catch if you stop to think."

"AJ, you seem like a really nice guy, but it's obvious to me that you are doing some type of drug because your eyes are red and glassy all the time. I will go, but you have to promise that you are straight up and not messing with that stuff while you are around me."

"Reba, I do some weed at times, but what's wrong with that?"

"It may be Okay to you but it's wrong for me, and I want no part of it," Reba shot back.

"Okay, Okay, Reba. I'm straight, and I haven't had a smoke for a long time."

"By the way, AJ, aren't you dating someone named Ashley? Why not have her meet you for a bite to eat, and Lord knows you seem to have the hots for that Faye person, so why not her?"

How did Reba know about Ashley? And here she go again with that Faye stuff. I never once mentioned Ashley to her, so how did she know? This woman must be working for CSI Chicago or something.

"Ah! Reba, Ashley and I are just good friends, and we go out sometimes but nothing serious. You know that a man has to have a little female companionship from time to time, and you wouldn't give a brother the time of day."

"AJ, between Faye and this Ashley person, you don't have time for me. But that's okay, we can still have a bite to eat and be friends."

Now I am really puzzled. How long has she known about Ashley and it's evident that she is not a fan of fabulous Faye.

After having a great evening with Reba, something was missing. As much as my whole existence was geared to getting Reba to notice me, now it seems somewhat anticlimactic. Had my brain and loins been fried by the mind-blowing sexual encounter with Faye? Had my attempt to get back at Faye for the beat-down by Shawn backfired on me? Whatever it was, I had to find out quickly, or once again I would blow this obvious opportunity with Reba that seem to be staring me in the face.

Since Faye had started to work at the dress shop, we had many more encounters. The thing that I liked about Faye was that she was a lot like me in that she wanted it when she wanted it and did not put any pressure on a brother. I had started limiting my time in the newspaper room after school because the summer was approaching, and I didn't have quite the desire to get a notch on my belt with Reba since I was spending so much time with Faye. How I managed all of this without pissing Ashley off, I don't know. Ashley had a very demanding schedule that allowed me to have quite a bit of free time. Many times, she was satisfied just getting a call from me after work because she was usually tired.

Just as that thought cleared my mind, the phone rang, and it was Ash. "What's up, Ash?"

"Oh, nothing, AJ. Why don't you come by tonight, and I will fix you a great dinner? Who knows what your desert will be. I am feeling the need for a little TLC, big boy, it's been a while."

That was definitely not what I needed after having another round with Faye just yesterday. "OK, Ash, it will be around seven before I can get there."

"That's fine with me as long as I see you, said Ash with excitement in her voice." Now what was I going to do? I didn't have the energy to go another round with anyone after the mind and body draining sex with Faye. I couldn't let Ash down though, because she has my back no matter what.

I decided to stop by the gym on my way home to try and work up an appetite for Ash's meal. Ash was not known for her cooking, but she could get by. I could expect some corn on the cob, black eyed peas, corn bread, and some Lee Roy the barnyard pimp. Ash could eat chicken every day.

Pumping iron gave me a degree of release from the world. It allows me to recharge my batteries after a long day. It clears my mind, and the musty scent challenges me to push much harder to clear my lungs of the bad habits that creep into my world from time to time. Seeing the ladies with the skintight workout clothes usually causes my testosterone levels to rise, but not this time. I took my precious time getting home to change before going to dinner with Ash.

I arrived at Ash's apartment at exactly 7:00 p.m. Before I could knock on the door, Ash, as if she were clairvoyant, opened it before my hand hit the wood. She must have been standing at the window watching for me. "Hello, AJ, I have missed you."

"Missed you too, Ash."

"Wow, AJ, I would have expected a little bit more than 'Me too, Ash,' since it's been a while since we last spent some quality time together."

"You are right, Ash, I just have had a lot on my mind lately with school and all and not having found a job yet for the summer."

"Come on in the kitchen with me, AJ, while I finish dinner."

As we strolled through her apartment, which was always immaculate, I could not help noticing the well-placed table setup, the wine glasses, and her finest china. Ash had a lot on her mind over and above the dinner. She was wearing a tight-fitting dress, one that I always loved to see her in. Though she did not possess the perfect-ten body of Faye or Reba, she used what she had well, and I truly loved being in her company. I was involved with three different women, all having different strengths. With Faye, it was totally sex; with Reba, it was class; and with Ash, it was support and security.

Everything was leading to a night of high expectations on Ash's part that I would be in a romantic mood. As she put the dinner on the table, she had this inquisitive look on her face. "AJ, you have been here for over an hour, and you have not kissed me as you usually do. What's wrong? Are you seeing someone else?"

"No, no, Ash, I am just tired tonight, haven't been sleeping well lately."

"Well, after dinner, I want you to go up to the bedroom, take a hot bath, and I am going to give you the best message that you have ever had. How does that sound?"

With a smile and a wink, I said, "Sounds great, Ash, I could use a good rubdown and a little shut-eye."

"AJ, I will put you to sleep all right." I knew what that meant, and I was not sure that I was up to it.

I took my time downing what was a pretty impressive dinner, and after a couple of glasses of Starmont Chardonnay, I was feeling somewhat revived. I have to admit, Ash was my favorite in bed until I was introduced to the major leagues by Faye. As I took my last bite of food, I noticed that Ash had taken her hair down and was looking pretty seductive. She lit two candles, came to the end of the table where I was sitting, slightly pulled up her dress just enough to allow her to straddle me, placed her face on my shoulder, and sat quietly for what seemed to be hours. She was happy just having me there. Now I felt worse than if I had not been able to perform up to standard. She was really what I needed, but greed had caused me to want more. More of what, I did not know.

Ash had dropped off into a deep sleep. I slowly eased her up, placed her comfortably in my arms, and carried her to the bedroom, where I undressed her to her panties and bra and covered her very comfortably. As I stood staring at her before I let myself out, a serene feeling came over me, causing me to crawl in bed next to her and lie quietly, just enjoying the quietness of the night and her body lying so peacefully. Though I never got my promised massage, I was spared of having to perform under less-than-perfect conditions.

This particular evening was a blessing in disguise because I really did have need of a good night's sleep. Morning came somewhat quicker than I had expected. I looked over at Ash, who was still in a deep sleep. I took a sheet from her notepad and left her a short note. "Ash, thanks for one of the best nights I have had in a long time. Even though I never got my massage, I am sure I'll have a rain check. I did spend the night and had one of my best nights of sleep for a long time. Thanks for a great dinner. See you soon, sweetheart. I still owe you, and I know you understand what I am referring to (smile)."

CHAPTER VII

The Summer Months

The end of the school term was finally here, and I knew this would be my last semester even though I had another two years to finish my degree in economics. I was destined for the unemployment line for the summer, while Reba was headed for her law classes at Harvard Law School. Reba was two years ahead of me in school and slowly but surely moving out of my life. Reba had not allowed me to even smell that nectar, and now she was about to leave Chicago for the sophisticated shores of the Ivy League. Surely those brothers without the mind clutter that I suffered from, would be able to finally get through that tough exterior of hers. I had to look at her as the one that got away.

As the summer months rolled by, I didn't see much of Reba because she was busy taking law courses, preparing for her entry into law school. I was on my way to the Dairy Queen with Chantal when I received a call from Reba. Her message was that she would be leaving Chicago on Monday and that she wanted to say good-bye. Why was I kidding myself? Reba was well beyond my reach. Why spend the time saying good-bye to her when there was a great possibility that it would be the last time I would lay eyes on her?

Against my better judgment, I agreed to meet her at the airport. After all, she had been a great friend, and I really enjoyed her company without there being any physical contact. Being late as I usually am, I figured that Reba would have gone through security because there was only forty five minutes until her flight was to leave.

As I approached the ticketing area, Reba called to me. "AJ, over here, hurry or I will be late. I didn't want to leave without saying good bye."

"Thanks, Reba, I will miss you. Go on over to the Ivy League and make us proud."

"I will miss you also, AJ, but just one thing you should always remember: Don't make assumptions because they may be wrong. You should go after what is important to you, if you know what I mean." Maybe, at some point, I would understand what she meant by that statement.

With that, Reba kissed me on each jaw and, with both hands on my face, kissed me tenderly like I had dreamed of for a long time. Her lips were so soft and sweet that they reminded me of the Krispy Kreme donuts when they come right out of the oven. They just melt in your mouth. I was standing there as if I didn't know what to do. Why was I so shy with her after she had given me signs that she cared? "AJ, we will see each other again, I promise," said Reba as she walked toward security. She had a look of really not wanting to leave, and for some reason, I was paralyzed and acting as if it meant nothing to me. As she disappeared into the corridor of the gateway to the plane, I suddenly realized that the opportunity that I had waited for such a long time had walked out of my life and into a world more fit to her pedigree.

I spent the first weeks of the school break looking for employment. Man, it was tough out there, and I needed some quick cash. As I was leaving the beauty shop where Moms worked, a black Mercedes 500SL pulled up beside me. The tinted window rolled slowly down, and a booming voice pierced the air. "What's up, AJ? It's been a long time, my vanilla-wafer brother."

I stooped to see who was in the backseat, and lo and behold, it was Cat Daddy. I hadn't seen him since high school. "What's up yourself,

Cat? You are rolling large these days, my well-dressed brother. It seems that you have done something right or . . . wrong."

Cat just peered out of the dark backseat with a smile worth solid gold. In fact, his grill was solid gold. "Brother AJ, what I do at night allows me to roll big during the day. I am in human resources, my inquisitive friend. I am in the people business, hahaha." I decided to let things lay just where they had fallen. The dudes surrounding him were definitely not his personal secretaries, and the heat on their belts did give me an idea of what business he was in. "Look, AJ, the word on the street is that you are looking for a gig while you are out of your precious college, is that true?"

"Ah, yes, but I am cool."

"Listen, AJ, we were always tight, and I want to help a brother out. I have a little job I want you to do for me. When it's over, there are ten big ones in it for you. What do you say?"

"What kind of job commands that type of scratch, Cat?"

"Look, AJ, you don't even have to know any details. I just need you to take this little box to the Makline Building on 24th and put it in the hands of a guy by the name of David Sorenson. His office is on the 5th floor. As you get off the elevator, turn right and go straight to the back of the building. You will see a set of double glass doors. Go through them and his office is on the right."

"May I ask who this David Sorenson is?"

"You may not. Now do we have a deal or what? If you decide not to take the 10 K, I will get it done, AJ. I just wanted to help a friend in need."

I knew this did not smell right, but ten big ones could give me a little independence and a way out of mom and dad's space.

"AJ, I don't have a lot of time, what's the word?"

"Okay, Okay. Give me the package, and I will make the drop. I am doing this for old times, Cat."

"I knew you would help an old friend, AJ. Now when you make the drop, call me at this number." The thug sitting in the front seat handed me a card with the number to call.

The building was just two blocks over and in walking distance. As I walked slowly north on Ventura Avenue, my stomach was turning in knots, knowing that something wasn't right. Why couldn't he make the drop himself? What was I getting myself into? I knew this was wrong, so why was I doing it?

As I walked into the Makline Building, an eerie feeling came over me, but I had committed and I was going through with it. It seemed as if everyone knew what I was there for because they seemed to focus on me. Or was it my imagination getting the best of me? I proceeded to the elevator, pressed the button for the 5th floor, and the ride seemed to last an eternity. As I looked for the double glass doors, my nerves were getting the best of me. Halfway down the hall, I stopped looked around and nervously continues down the corridor. Sweat was popping off my brow as if I had just come in out of the rain." Get it together, AJ," I said to myself. "Just walk in, identify Mr. Sorenson, drop the package, and be gone." As I walked into the office, the secretary asked whether I had an appointment. "No, I don't, but I wanted to drop this package off to Mr. Sorenson. I think he is expecting it."

"Okay, I will take it."

"With all due respect, I have to deliver it to Mr. Sorenson."

Without further argument, she got on the phone. "Mr. Sorenson, there is a man here with a package for you."

"Thanks, Sherri, I will be right out." As Mr. Sorenson took the package, two men dressed to the nines came out of his office and took the package. Mr. Sorenson was part of a drug sting operation to identify the source of what proved to be a sophisticated meth ring operating in the area, and there I was, caught up in it with no place to go and no explanation of my involvement.

"Young man, please step into the office," said one of the detectives. Once in the office, he started by saying, "Make it easy on yourself and tell us your source. Are you involved or did someone give you this package?"

"Sir, I don't know what you mean. I was asked to deliver a package to Mr. Sorenson, and that's what I did."

"You always drop packages off for people without asking questions?"

"No, sir, I know this individual, and I was doing him a favor."

"Well, young man, he didn't do you any favors. Who is the person that asked you to drop off the package?"

I knew that was going to be the next question. If I tell, I get Cat in trouble, and if I don't, I am subject to be arrested. "Sir, the only thing that I can tell you is that we call him Cat. I am not sure what his real name is. We have called him Cat since we were kids."

"Do you know where he lives?"

"No, sir, we just would hang out together when we were in high school."

"Young man, this package contains some of the most powerful meth on the street. We are going to have to take you down to the station until you can give us a little more than you are giving."

Now what do I do? I was not about to give them the number that Cat had given me, but I can't take the hit for this. He got me involved in something that I knew had to be wrong, but I did it anyway. They spared me the embarrassment of handcuffing me, but I was going to be booked nevertheless. I had one call per the law, and I was going to call Cat. Getting into the black SUV was something like you see if the movies. I should have followed my intuition and stayed clear of what I knew was something I had a feeling was wrong. The long drive to the station was one of the most reflective moments of my life. I walked into the station with the two dark suited investigators on each side of me and at that moment, I felt dirty, like a criminal.

After booking was complete, I was asked if I wanted to make a call. They moved me into a small room with a phone, a table, and two chairs. They had not asked me to empty my pockets, so I still had the card from Cat. I dialed the number, and it rang and rang with no answer. Finally, Cat answered. "What's up, AJ? Did you take care of business for me?"

"Cat, I am in jail. You got me caught up in a sting, man. What am I gonna do?"

"Shit, AJ, how the hell did that happen?"

"Evidently, they have been watching Sorenson, and they may be watching you."

"AJ, what did you tell them, man?"

"I told them that you asked me to drop off a package and that's all I knew."

"Did you give them my name?"

"No, I didn't, because I don't even know your name. That's why I am down here. They think I am a part of some drug ring. Please tell me that you are not involved in drugs, Cat."

"AJ, I am so sorry, man. I didn't intend for this to happen. Give me time to figure this out."

"Yea, but in the meantime, I am stuck here. What am I going to tell my parents?"

At that point, the phone went dead. I am not worried so much about tonight because my parents know that I often stay over at Ash's place, but what happens tomorrow? As I hung up the phone, the detective came in to see if I could give them any more information. After telling them that I had told them all that I knew, I was led to a cell where I stayed until the next morning.

I paced in that small cell all night. I didn't get a wink of sleep. At about 7:00 a.m., the detective came in and told me that I was going to be allowed to leave because a man had come in and admitted to giving me the package. The man's name was Cecil A. Turner. As I walked through the booking room, I saw Cat sitting with two officers. He looked over and acknowledged me with a nod. Cat had turned himself in to get me out of this mess. Though I had dodged a direct hit, I was still an accessory, and that would go on my record. Cat had told them that I was just doing him a favor and that I had nothing to do with anything else. The detective released me with a warning. "Young man, let this be a lesson to you. Never allow anyone to use you in that manner, no matter friend or foe."

"Yes, sir, I realized that the request was a little suspect, but he was a friend and I trusted him. Never again."

It did prove that Cat was really a friend because he didn't have to expose himself and there would have been nothing that I could have done about it. Cecil A. Turner. *C-A-T.* I finally knew his name, but what a way to find out. He was later convicted of distribution of illegal drugs and served two years in the Cook County Jail. If moms knew what had transpired, it would absolutely kill her, and she would have kill me. The thing I hated most, other than my now having a record, was not being able to spend the ten big ones that had been promised by Cat. Under the circumstances, I am fortunate to have my freedom. It was a close call.

Now, getting a good job where they would do a thorough background check would be impossible. Walking in and out of places and being told that they had no opportunities really made a career in basketball even more appealing. Having people less qualified than I was tell me that I lack experience just rubbed me the wrong way. Many of these brothers from another mother couldn't recognize talent if it was wrapped around their worthless necks. Flipping hamburgers and wearing those sissy-ass uniforms is not my idea of employment, but a brother needs a job and I was ready to do most anything, on the legal side, to earn some dough.

As I walked toward downtown with an old, broken-down fence on my left, I noticed an advertisement for help at Sammy's Car Wash and Auto Repair hanging precariously on one board. Below the weathered writing was a number to call. Now would come the challenge of finding a phone booth in an area where not only the phone book would usually be missing, but sometimes the phone itself. These wine heads around Chicago would try to sell anything to get a bottle of Ripple or some cough syrup. As I turned the corner, headed in the direction of the car wash, a booth was across the street at the next corner. I hurried to cross the street, and just as I started to step off the curb, a cab nearly ran me over. A voice came from the cab, cursing me out in French or German or something.

After finally negotiating the busy avenue, I was lucky to find the phone intact. I dialed the number that was on the poster, and a young lady with a sultry voice answered. For the first time, I felt that employment was within my reach, especially if a woman was to make the decision.

"Hello, may I help you?"

"Yes" was the response from the other end. "Yes, my name is August James, and I noticed that you had openings at the car wash, is that correct?"

"Yes, sir, we do. What you need to do is come down and fill out an application as soon as possible because there are only a few openings left."

Now how would I get there in time to make this happen? The car wash was eight blocks away, and they were to close in thirty minutes. I had to get on my get-dyap to make it in time. As fast as I was, it was still a challenge. I made it with about five minutes to spare. I entered the front door and walked toward a desk in the far corner of the room. A young redhead greeted me with a smile and asked if I was the gentlemen who had called.

"Yes, I am August James, but all my friends call me AJ, and that's what I want you to call me because I feel already that we will be friends. So when can I start?" I have to admit that I was on my game today. There was no way she could recover from that smooth cellophane that I had just wrapped around her.

She smiled back, not being able to look me in the eyes. I knew then that I was in. "Sir . . . I mean, AJ," she said shyly. "Have you ever worked in a car wash before?"

"I have, if you think that would help," I said as I leaned in toward her.

"But sir, I am sorry, I mean . . . AJ, my boss is looking for dependable, experienced workers because we have been losing business because of the quality of our service."

"What's your name?" I said.

"My name is Wanda."

"Well, pleased to meet you, Wanda, and because time is short and I know you have to close, let's do this. You need workers and I need a job, and I am sure you won't be disappointed with the quality of any of my work," I said as I gave her my patented smile and wink.

Her next words were "Okay, I don't know why I am doing this, but if anyone asks, you have worked at a car wash before, so I won't get in trouble. When can you start?"

I said to her, "I just did."

She knew exactly why she was doing it. She wanted some of this vanilla chocolate, and she knew it. What she said was music to my ears. Finally, I can buy a lady some dinner, put some petro in my ride, and save a buck or two. Maybe Ashley can keep her mouth off of a brother for asking for a loan or two. She had really propped the old boy up in his time of need, and now maybe I can return the favor.

I couldn't wait to get up the next morning to go to my first gig. I showered, did my daily routine, and headed for the car wash. I could drive now because now I can put some petro in my tank. I backed out of the garage to Luther Vandross singing "Let's Make Tonight the Night," and I was sailing on cloud nine.

As I entered the parking lot, I saw Wanda getting out of a blue Toyota, and some guy was trying to kiss her good-bye, but she nixed his effort and hurried to the side door of the carwash as he drove away. "Wanda," I called out. "It's me, AJ . . . here live and in living color. I just wanted to thank you for what you did yesterday, and I won't let you down, I promise."

She smiled with a suggestive bite of the bottom lip and responded with "I hope not, I really hope not." There was more in that second "hope not" than meets the eye. That girl was coming on to me big time, and I have to admit, she was not hard on the eyes and had two nice apples following her in that tight dress she was wearing.

The first day was a drag because there was very little traffic, but the second day was a different story. They worked my butt off. As I returned home after my day on the job, Chantal met me at the door, letting me know that Ashley had called. I picked up the phone to dial Ashley because I had made some nice tips and I could take her out for a nightcap and finally follow up on what we should have done at dinner. "Hello, Ash, Chantal told me that you had called. What's up?"

"Oh, nothing, AJ, just wanted to say how proud I am that you are working and enjoying your new job."

"Yes, Ash, it feels good to be working though it's only a minimum wage job, but it will allow me to save a bit and not mooch off you so much. You know a brother has to contribute something."

"That's cool, AJ, I am just happy that you are happy."

"Ash, want to go out for a drink or something?"

"Thanks, AJ, I would love to, but I have an early start tomorrow, and it's my long day, so I am turning in early. Maybe I can come by and have lunch on Friday?"

"Yeah, that's cool . . . OK, sleep well, and see you on Friday." The rest of the week was uneventful other than having flirtation sessions with Wanda. She was chumping it to bits to get close to me and I wanted to make her wait.

On Friday at lunch, Ash pulled up in her cream-colored Infinity, looking fine to the nine. As I greeted her with a slight kiss on the jaw as I got in on the passenger side, I could see Wanda looking through the window as we pulled out.

After a nice lunch with Ashley, she dropped me off, giving me a wave as she left. As I headed toward the changing room, a voice came from near the office area. "AJ, are you married, or was that your girlfriend?"

"Oh, what's up, Wanda? No, that was a friend of mine. We see each other from time to time."

"Oh . . . Is it the type of relationship that would prevent you from seeing someone else sometimes?" I smiled and said," Do you have someone in mind?" "What if I do AJ?

"Wanda, I didn't know you wanted to go out with me. What about the dude who drops you off every day?"

"I am letting him hang around until I say no. AJ, you tell me yes . . . I'll tell him no."

"We will see, Wanda, but be careful what you ask for pretty lady."

"AJ, whatever you throw I can catch. So you marinate on that for a while my handsome friend." Wanda was pushing my button, and she knew it. We both knew that things had to come to a head sooner or later.

I had decided not to enter the fall semester because the money was not that good plus I wanted to give the parent's pocket a break. The little I was making hustling at the car wash was but kept grits and biscuits on the table, which was my contribution. After working for a considerable time at the car wash, I had finally saved enough money to get my own place. Moms wouldn't let Chantal come to live with me because she thought me to be too unstable. She was right, if I have to say so myself. I try to spend as much time with Chantal as possible. I was determined that she would be like Reba and attend one of the premier schools.

The years had hurried by, and hanging out with Pookie and Maurice had become my pastime. Pookie was my best friend growing up, and I had not laid eyes on the sucker during the semester. During my time at school, Pookie would not come around because he felt uncomfortable around the college crowd. It was usual for Pookie to be underfoot, but for the last week since classes stopped, I had not seen hide nor hair of that pest of a so-called friend. He must have finally found someone who was willing to put up with his trifling butt other than me. He carried around a beat-up old mobile phone, but either the thing never works or it's strictly for show. It's like people who send flowers to themselves to make people think that someone cares. Pookie is one of those individuals that were dropped on their heads at birth and were dropkicked across the room because they were so damn ugly. I don't discriminate against ugly. If I did, Pookie would not be in my friend stable because he is, to say the least, a homely sucker. Pookie dropped out of kindergarten, so he wasn't into the school thing.

I was now well-entrenched in a position at Sammy's Car Wash. It was nearing lunch time, and I was dead-tired from smiling at these honkies and uppity blacks coming through the car wash with their Benzes, BMWs, and Caddies. Many of them were just one unfortunate incident away from being right here in this car wash, getting dirty, and smelling like old soap, just like me.

As the irritating whistle sounded for my one-hour lunch break, here came Pookie, rushing toward me with a panicked look on that ugly face of his.

"Man, what ails you?" I asked.

"Listen, AJ, I overheard this dude mentioning your name, and he seemed mighty pissed."

"Pissed about what? Did you know him, Pookie?"

"Hell no, man, I could not get a good look at him because of his hoodie, but what I did see of him, I didn't recognize. All I know is, he was a big dude with light skin. The dude could have been white, for all I know. Man, he was shouting, cussing, and gesturing in a very threatening way. AJ, were you messing with this dud e's lady or something?"

"Go on, Pookie, I hadn't done nothing to nobody. You must have heard it wrong."

"AJ, how many people do you know around here named AJ? You better watch your back, my trusting and most naive brother."

"Pookie, shut the hell up. Man, you need to take something for that diarrhea of the mouth. You been talking since you stumbled your raggedy ass in here. Now do you want something to eat or what? You are wasting my time."

"All right, Mista Know-Nothing . . ."

"Pookie, it's Know-It-All, not Know-Nothing. Man, you are a trip."

Pookie and I went over to a little greasy spoon restaurant just across Main Street to get a sandwich and a cup of coffee. I knew he would show up around lunchtime to get a free meal. Though I didn't let Pookie know it, my mind began to wonder about who was asking about me. I have never had issues with anyone other than a small riff with a dude in jail when I was convicted of shoplifting a few years back. I had to whip a dude's tail because he was trying to bitch me out. He threatened to get even with me when he got out, but I heard that he was canceled by a .357 magnum in the hands of his old lady for abusing her. Other than that incident, old AJ has kept his nose clean. There was the Shawn ordeal, but that white boy didn't want any more of me. He was a little embarrassed that I was able to trump him with that fine Faye. That's been several years ago, so I know that dude is over that by now. I see him around town with a fine, big-legged white girl, so he must have gotten over Faye. She has to be special because forgetting Faye ain't easy. Maybe he finally realized that he was out of his league.

As the months hurried by, I had yet to decide to finish my last year at Northwestern. I had gotten into a little trouble selling drugs trying to make ends meet a few years back, and that shit was on my record now. A stupid mistake like that will unfortunately follow me for the rest of my life. Luckily, I was given a short sentence because of my past good record and only had to spend a few months in the joint and was allowed to walk because of good behavior. Faye and I would see each other from time to time for a roll in the sack but she was not the one that

I felt would be a long term relationship. I still had my old dependable Ask who stood by me through thick and thin.

The money at the car wash was weak, but it kept the old boy in sneakers and gas in my car. I was able to put aside ten percent from my paycheck, plus the tips had given me enough to maintain my apartment. Four years had gone by, and I was still washing cars and putting a few dollars away for emergencies, but more importantly, I had not been focused and had not finished my last year at Northwestern. By dropping out for such a long time, it really hindered my chances to build toward a future in the NBA.

Just as I took the last bite of the heart attack burger, the phone rang. I had to clean my hands because of the mustard, catsup, and grease that poured from the waxed paper used to keep the paper bag from getting soaked. Viewing the screen and not recognizing the number, I decided to let it go into voicemail. It was a long-distance call, and my bill was high enough as it was. A few minutes later, the phone rang again. Now who could want me that bad to keep calling me like this? As I picked up the phone, a familiar voice said, "AJ, it's me, Reba, don't you remember?"

"Oh yes, yes, Reba, how are you?" Now I'm stuck. "It's been a long time, girl. I thought that you had forgotten us poor folks back here in Chicago."

"AJ, why haven't I heard from you? You said that you would keep in touch."

"Well, Reba, I got busy, and you know that a brother has to make a living."

"So tell me, AJ, what are you doing these days? You didn't even think to invite me to graduation."

"Well, Reba, I did not get around to graduating yet, and life came in conflict with my finishing school, but I still plan to though." Reba was an extraordinary person, but I had blown the relationship during my pot-smoking, macking days back at Northwestern. She was my perfect dream of a woman back then, and I had let her slip right through my fingers. Man, she had a body that had perfection written all over it and legs that Tina Turner would be jealous of. She was never one to chase after guys because the girl was focused on her future, which I was not to be a part of. One thing about Reba is that she is no-nonsense, and she didn't play. When she got wind of my smoking that funny weed, she made it clear that we were headed in different directions and dropped me like a Muhammad Ali right cross.

As I took my hand from over the phone to acknowledge her, I realized that she had been right all along. She had told me that I wouldn't amount to nothing because of my habits, and nothing was what I had become. I cleared my throat and spoke again. "Reba, where are you?"

"I am in Indianapolis for a legal conference, and you crossed my mind. I will be here for a few days if you want to get together for a few drinks and catch up. It's only a short ride from Chicago."

"Yeah, Reba . . . I know, but it's a bad time for me. My pops has been ill, and I have to stay close in case he or Moms needs something. With Moms working and everything, I need to stay close in case there is an emergency." I was lying my ass off, but what else can I do? I couldn't let her know what a loser I had become.

I really wanted to see Reba and wrap my arms around those great curves of hers, but I knew better. How could I face her with my life being in the shambles that it is? How did she look after four years, and was she giving that nectar to any of those Ivy League guys? "Reba, let me call you later to let you know if we can meet?"

"AJ, don't play with me now. I expect you to keep your promise and call me back."

"I will, Reba, I promise." I closed the lid on my cell phone. I breathed a brief sigh of relief because I dodged a bullet on that one, but what do I do now? Do I call her back or not?

"AJ, you been sitting here and fat mouthing with everyone as if I wasn't here. Who the hell is Reba anyway," said Pookie. "Don't remember you talking about her. You been holding out on old Pookie."

"Man, that was one that I let slip through my fingers back during my last semester in college. She's in Indy and wants me to come over to see her while she is there."

"You going?" said Pookie.

"Hell to the no, man! You must be tripping. Reba was well out of my league then and even more so now, and I would be embarrassed to just hold a conversation with her. What would I say, "Oh, by the way, Reba, I work in a car wash? Notwithstanding the fact that Ashley would murder-rise a brother. Ashley has been too good to me to screw up. Reba can tempt the most honest brother with what she has. She is gorgeous and brainy and is the type of woman who has high expectations of herself as well as those she deal with."

"AJ, Ashley has been your life line all this time so slow your roll with these other side pieces," Said Pookie. If you don't I may have to put a bug in Ash's ear about my philandering friend. I swear I will tell her AJ."

"Tell her what? Pookie, are you out of your crazy-ass mind?"

"That's right, AJ, I will sing like a bird in a window on Sunday morning," said Pookie.

"Pookie, don't play, I got enough trouble as it is, and I definitely don't need your ass screwing things up more for me with Ash."

I wolfed down part of the sandwich and quickly hurried back to finish my shift, leaving Pookie sucking down French fries like a vacuum cleaner. I couldn't wait until 5:00 p.m. to get away from this hellhole. As I washed my last car of the evening, a 2008 Lexus, I noticed a car parked across the street from the car wash. As I stood gazing at the late-model red Ford Mustang with twenty-twos, the driver slowly pulled off and seemed to point in my direction. It was probably nothing but my imagination playing tricks on me. I remembered that Shawn had pointed at me and Faye in that same manner, but that dude couldn't be holding a grudge that long. Or could he? Off in the distance, it did seem like a white boy.

Finally, the hour was at hand, and I quickly dried my hands, placed my equipment in the locker, and carefully slid my size 12 feet out of the boots so that my socks would stay on. They were a little soggy from standing in water all day. I tried to hurry to the time clock before there was a line. I knew that I had to speed it up because the midtown bus waits for no mother's son. Though, I would drive my car sometimes, because of traffic, it was sometimes more economically sound to take the bus.

I finally arrived at the bus stop with about five minutes to spare. The driver was beginning to close the doors when he heard me banging on the back door. I stepped onto the bus with a sigh of relief because I definitely didn't want to be stranded on that side of town waiting thirty minutes for the next bus. It would eat into my little stash of money to have to grab a cab, so I was pleased that the driver had it in his heart to open the door.

I remembered that Reba was expecting a call, and as much as I wanted to see her, I knew that it was impossible. I can't lie to Reba; she could see right through me. I will put off calling her until later when I get home. As I boarded the midtown bus headed home after an evening of washing cars for people who didn't even know I existed, I decided to sit in a seat nearest to the back door so that I could have a good view of the folks getting on and off the bus. What Pookie was saying was starting to work on my mind. Maybe there is someone out there that would like to see me with dire in my face.

It was 6:00 p.m. now, and riding the midtown bus was akin to getting combat pay for serving in Vietnam. Every slimy creature that had crawled from underneath every rock in the city seemed to find their way to this midtown bus route. As I sat dreading even going home to the dreary apartment, I slowly slid my hand into my pocket to see how I had done with the evening tips from busting my behind, washing cars for people who literally hate me. These losers not only hate you because of your race, they look down their noses because we at the car wash was not at their socio-economic level. A quarter fell to the floor and rolled about two feet and rested under a seat across the aisle. Damn, I can't afford to lose a dime, so I tucked the rest back in my pocket and moved quickly to rescue my quarter.

Once back in my seat, I carefully removed the change again without dropping anything this time. To my surprise, I had been blessed with tips totaling ninety-five dollars and thirty-five cents . It was my best day ever at the car wash. The people who get their cars washed at Sammy's were pretty good tippers. It was nothing for them to drop a ten on a brother, so sometimes I did more in tips than in my paycheck it seemed.

The ninety-five dollars would come in handy until I got my check on Friday. In fact, it was about as much as I got in my regular check anyway. It was almost embarrassing to admit that I was settling for a minimum wage job, but it is what it is. I am sure that Reba would be proud of me. Yeah, right! A man's gotta do what a man's gotta do to get along in this ghetto of a world. Why did I put up with this meager existence when there are better options out there for me?

I continued to observe the cliental that got on and off the bus. There was the old lady who always stood even when the bus had plenty seats. She always had a large dirty brown bad with what I thought to be all of her worldly possessions. Then there was the nerd who would always sit behind to bus driver as if to say, "No one will bother me here". He always had a book in his hand which seemed to be the story of Mohammed Ali. He would read a few pages and glance up to see if he was being noticed. Then sitting just to the right of the standing bag lady was the pretty young lady with long black flowing hair, tight blue jeans with a stripe down the side, Jordan sneakers and and a New York Yankees cap which accented her outfit. She had the look of someone who regretted having to go where ever she was headed. She seemed sad and lonely but who knows what demons are chasing each of us. I am sure each of these individuals, like me, had their own stories

I had blown every opportunity to make something out of myself by dropping out of school, and now I was washing cars for a lousy living with no end in sight. I knew the importance of an education, but I had no one constantly reminding me, so I took the easy way out. I was good at basketball, baseball, and track, but the pull of the streets was stronger than any of my God-given talents. How could I motivate myself to go back to school when there were people with degrees working with me at the car wash. Unemployment was high because of the economy in Chicago? The little hope that I had to eventually get out of this rat hole was being challenged by reality as life played these war games with me.

As my bus crossed Pine Avenue, I could see that this was not going to be a pleasant evening. A soft mist had started to cover the streets, which normally is a sure indicator in the Windy City that the worst weather was yet to come. The wind had started to move the bus from side to side, and sheets of paper and trash could be seen flying by the window. As we passed vacant lots, these miniature tornadoes could be seen stirring up more of the trash and garbage lying in the gutters and on the sidewalks. This was reminiscent of the dust storms I remembered seeing rumbling across the dusty roads at grandma's house down in New Orleans when I was a kid. Sometimes I wished I could go back to that time when there were no worries, few responsibilities, and always plenty to eat on the table. That seem to be so long ago now.

My phone rang again and I knew it was Reba. I didn't even bother to look at the screen, nor did I answer it. As my conscience tugged at me, I decided to return the call to Reba and face the music because it wasn't her fault that I was struggling with my self-inflicted war within. But as I gazed down at the phone screen, I realized that it was Ashley who had called and not Reba. Before I return the call to Ash, I decided to call Reba and tell her that I would meet her for a drink on Friday. Since she had made the effort to keep in touch with me, I could at least have a drink with her. I dialed the number, still unsure of what I would say. The phone rang at least seven times, and just as I had decided to hang up, Reba picked up.

"Hello, is that you AJ?"

There was a silent pause on my part because fear was creeping in, slowly but surely.

"AJ, is that you?"

"Oh, yes, yes, Reba, it's me. How are you?"

"Thanks for calling me back. I really wanted to hear from you. Now make me very happy by telling me that you are on your way to Indy, please, please."

"Well, Reba, I do want to see you and catch up, so what about Friday? I will try to get there around 8:00 p.m., does that work?"

"Anytime you get here works for me, stated an excited Reba."

Now I am cautious but carrying a grin from ear to ear because she was excited to see me. Maybe a little of the attraction that was always there between Reba and me still had a little of its magic.

I was beginning to warm up to the idea because of the excitement in her voice. I was on cloud nine, but unknowingly, the cloud was about to burst and deliver a downpour that would have me waterlogged. "OK, Reba, I will see you Friday." As I hung up from Reba feeling good about myself, I quickly phoned Ashley to let her know that I would be at my flat soon and would call her. Ashley picked up on the first ring.

"AJ, why haven't I heard from you all day?"

"Ah, Ash, give a brother a break. It's been a long day, and I did pretty good on my tips today. Maybe we can go out and get some barbeque later."

"I don't want to go anywhere in this weather. What I was calling about was my wing at the hospital is having a recognition celebration and Roast for one of the doctors who is retiring, and I really want you to go with me. I don't bother you a lot about this type thing but this one is really important to me, AJ, because he has been really supportive of me and has helped me tremendously over the years with my career."

"When is it, Ash?"

"It's this Friday at the Ritz Carlton, and you know I love that place. You can spring for a massage if you want to."

"Girl, now you are really tripping. Where the hell will I get enough money to pay for a massage at that place? You sure it is this Friday?"

"Yes, it is this Friday. Do you have something better to do? You never take me anywhere, so I hope you are not even thinking about trying to get out of it."

My stomach started to do flips. How did I get myself into this mess? Of all times for her to go out with those stuffed shirts that she works with, she had to pick the same day that I had committed to meet Reba in Indy. "Ash, Ash, Ash—" I pretended to have a bad connection and hung up so I would have time to think. It was either the girl that had been in my corner through thick and thin over the years or the girl who I had dreamed about having a close relationship with since college. What a mess I had gotten myself into. My day had gone from bad to a friggin tsunami.

Ashley was my girl for now. She and I had been dating on and off for the past five years, and she picked me up after the unfortunate run-in with the law. She did not judge me and always encouraged me to improve myself. She was a nurse's aide at Mercy Hospital and Medical

Center across town. She is a smart, dedicated street girl but did have a lot of class about her and a temper something fierce. When she got angry, it lasted for a long time, which affected my love life and the ability to knock the hell out of those boots, if you get my drift. Her family always thought that I was no good for her, but I had worked hard to get into their favor. Now when they find out about this, and she will tell them, I will be right back at square one. (I don't know what it is about us men, but we tend to take adventure and living on the edge more seriously than making common sense decisions.)

The bus driver stopped to let a few passengers off and a few on at each stop along the route. The night seemed uneventful so far, and that was completely fine with me. The normal cast of Neanderthals must have been aware of the approaching weather and had opted to stay in their caves. As the bus approached 15th and Madison, the wind started to swirl harder and harder, when suddenly I could hear the huge raindrops bouncing off the top of the bus. The drops were so large that it sounded like it was hailing. The sky opened up and the rain came down in buckets it seemed, and lightning seemed to strike the buildings just up ahead of us. Why couldn't God have just waited a few more minutes to give me a chance to get home? The gall of me to even think that I can question God's work! One thing that always stuck with me was my grandmother telling us to unplug all of the electrical stuff in the house like the toaster, the TV, and the stereo, and sit quietly while the Almighty does his work. "So I am sorry God for even attempting to question your wisdom, please forgive me."

The bus rocked and swerved in the downpour as sheets of water scattered people on the sidewalks The bus finally arrived at my stop, and as I stepped off, I couldn't help but get the eerie feeling that I was being watched. It was only a passing feeling though, because no one cared about me other than my family and I had no grudge with anybody.

I did still owe a debt from my days of smoking that funny weed, but the dealer that I was working with had long been jailed for money laundering and possession of over a quarter million dollars in cocaine. That white horse has been the death of many a dealer and their users. I didn't want that to be my fate so I decided to clean up my act. I wonder if my past is coming back to haunt me. I surely hope not, because I have been clean and have no desire to return to smoking that devil weed ever again. It still sometimes calls my name, but believe me, I ain't listening no more.

The bus stop was approximately three blocks from my flat, so I had to make a mad dash toward home before I was totally waterlogged. I took off all my jewelry before leaving the bus to keep the lightning from striking me. As I ran for home, the water splashing from my shoes hitting the sidewalk was so intense that it had started to fill my Kmart special sneakers. My running and the wet shoes made it sound as if I had rubber galoshes on.

I finally reached the porch which had a small stoop over it to shield the front door from the devastating summer sun. Here in Chicago, very little can shield a person from the cold and heartless winters or the relentlessly hot summers that cause every bone in your body to ache like a terrible case of pneumonia in the winter and feel like fried chicken in the sweltering heat of the summer.

As I stood under the stoop and fumbled for my door keys, that feeling hit me again. It was stronger than ever this time. Why was I feeling as if I was being watched? I turned and did a quick scan of the immediate area, but everything seemed Okay, with the exception of the weather taking a turn for the worse. Finally getting the key in the door and pushing to get inside gave me some relief, but I was soaked from head to toe. As I climbed the inner stairs to my front door, I could hear my stomach growling, after only eating that grease burger and fries for lunch. The thought hit me that it would have been great getting home to a cozy house and a warm meal, but quickly I pinched myself and woke up from that dream. I used to go to mama's house after work to get a meal, but Mama had not fixed a meal since she started to ride the white horse. As for my pops, he was so wasted by the time he got home that food was the furthest thing from his pickled mind. My hunger pains would continue until the weather let up and I was able to go down the street to McDonalds or convince Ashley to go with me for barbeque.

As I stepped into the flat, it gave me little comfort from the feeling that had come over me. I immediately took off my sneakers and poured the water into a bucket that was near the door. I took off my socks and clothes and put on my bathrobe. I took a few deep breaths, lit a cigarette, and strolled to the window to see who else had fallen victim to the elements as I had. While near the window, I checked the messages on the house phone. The first one that came up was Ashley asking me to call as soon as I got in the door. I could tell by the tone of her voice that she was not happy that I had not answered her question and had not finished the conversation. I picked up the phone to call her, without knowing what to say. I was playing Russian roulette with my life and my relationship with Ashley, but nothing would keep me from something that I had dreamed about ever since Reba left. I desperately wanted to see Reba and rekindle, if only for a moment, what we had before.

The phone started to ring, and immediately Ash picked up. "AJ, what took you so long to call me, and why did you hang up on me?"

"Girl, quit tripping. We had a bad connection, and I didn't try to call back because the weather was getting worse and I wanted to wait until I got home. I am calling you now right? So slow your roll!"

"What's this attitude I am hearing from you, AJ? Do I detect an attitude?"

"Nah, Ash, but, but . . ."

"But what, AJ?"

"Ash, I can't go to the Ritz with you on Friday 'cause I have to go to Indy to see an old buddy of mine. I had promised him that I would visit when he passed through, and he is coming in on Friday. That's what I was trying to tell you when we were talking before, but we were cut off."

"Why you never told me about this before now with your trifling ass, and what buddy are you lying about? I know you didn't just plan this today. If you didn't want to go to the event with me, why didn't you just man up and say it? Don't play me, AJ. I don't ask you for much, but this is important to me and you continue to play games after all we have been through."

"Come on, Ash, you remember Raymond Renolds who went off to play with the San Francisco 49ers. We called him Ray Ray when he was back on the block. I told you about him many times. That was a bad dude with the pigskin. He had been trying to get up with me every time he came through, and I was always tied up."

"AJ, you are tied up again, and I am not taking no for an answer. If you do not go with me to this . . . you will regret it with your lying ass and don't think for a minute that I am buying that Ray Ray shit. Whoever you are going to see, I hope it's worth it, because it could cost you a lot." Ash had just read me like a book. That's the Perry Mason shit coming out in Ash right now, I said to myself. It's like she reads my thoughts. I didn't want to lose her, but I wasn't going to give up an opportunity to see Reba again.

The old conscience was whipping my tail. The good devil on the right said, "AJ, stay your tail in Chicago and take Ash to the Ritz." The bad devil on the left shoulder said, "Man, this may be your last chance to tap Reba and hold those curves in the palms of your hands just one more time." Needless to say, the devil on the left shoulder won. Ash had been mad with me before and got over it, so what's different this time? I still didn't feel good about it.

The conversation continued with Ash, "Ash, would I do you like that? I wouldn't do it if I had not cancelled all the other hookups we tried to have. The brother is cool, and I hoped you would understand." Just then my ears were ringing from the sound of the phone hanging up on Ash's end. She was thoroughly pissed, and I was feeling like shit because I had lied to her again.

Reba was in Indy and ready to rekindle our old friendship, and I was heading into the perfect storm. I got up early Friday morning and headed to work knowing that the evening was hopefully going to be one to remember. I couldn't help but wonder what Ash would do about the Ritz; she had gone to events before without me. I had never experienced the anger like last night. The day seemed to drag by in anticipation of seeing Reba. Even the attitudes of the snobs and silver spooners did not affect me today. Nothing was going to ruin my mood . . . I thought. Little did I realize that Shawn was trying anything to get back at me for stealing some of Faye's nectar. He had found out where I was working and was setting the stage to hopefully suck me in to his little scheme.

Shawn had this thing about black girls and he pulled them into his web by paying the cost to be the boss.

Just a few blocks away, Shawn and one of his female friend by the name of Portia, a tall and well-stacked tender roni, were having a serious conversation that was to include me.

"Portia, what's up, girl, said Shawn? I see you haven't lost any of the spark that made you homecoming queen a few years ago, stated Shawn"

"Shawn, I am always going to keep all of this in the right place, if you know what I mean. It's a mean world out there, and these Chicago women are trying to get their hooks in any man who can walk upright. As for me, there must be something special about any man who rubs up against all of this, and that special thing is a job and plenty of money. These trifling-ass men here in Chicago want you to take care of them. Well, they have the wrong tree to bark up because they get nothing here."

"Portia, Portia . . . Some things never change. You still have as much piss and vinegar as you ever had."

"So, Shawn, to what do I owe this chance encounter? Knowing you, there is something up your sleeve, other than those muscular arms."

"Since you put it that way, I do have a favor to ask, and if you do it, we can spend a little time together just like old times. I am sure that I can make you smile like I did back in the day."

"White boy, please, the only reason I was smiling back then is because you spend the money on a girl, and my black solders didn't have even a closed bank account. Most of them couldn't help me if they wanted to. As far as your lovemaking, Shawn, I hope you have gotten more practice since then, my less-than-Nubian brother. By the way, weren't you and that hustler Faye an item? Don't tell me she kicked you to the curb."

"Girl, stop trippin', you don't give a bro a break for nothing. I did the kicking, but that's another story. This dude was undercutting me with Faye and embarrassed me in front of my boys, and he has to pay. No one threatens me with a weapon and lives to enjoy it."

"So, Shawn, what has that got to do with me? With your reputation of leaving bodies all over Chicago, what makes this one different?"

"Look, Portia, we have been friends for a long time, so do this one thing for me and you can call your price as long as it's not a car or something crazy expensive."

"Shawn, you are serious. Who is this masked man, and what do you want me to do with him?"

"Portia, I just want you to attract this dude to your nectar, and that should be easy, as fine a wine as you are. He will take the bait because this guy thinks he is God's gift to women and will screw a snake if you hold the head. When he gets an eyeful of your fine ass, he will flip out and do some crazy shit, which will fall right into my hands. I want you to get him to come to your apartment, and I will be waiting for his sorry ass with more than a big stick."

"Wait a minute. Don't be planning nothing in my apartment that will have the cops looking for me. Whatever you are planning had better be prior to his getting to my place, am I making myself clear? Shawn, I like you, white boy, but this shit I am not sure about. Who is this guy that's making your brain pregnant anyway?"

"His name is AJ, and he works at the car wash down the street. That sucker was tipping with Faye behind my back, and no one does me that way . . . No one."

"Shawn, it sounds to me like you are after the wrong person. He couldn't do anything that she didn't let him do."

"Don't worry, her time comes next, and it won't be pretty."

"OK, back to what's in it for me. I saw this mesmerizing fur jacket that cost $6,000 down at Gino's Furs that is out of my range, but I want it so bad. That's what I want, nothing more, nothing less. If I attract this AJ to my place, just make sure that I am not tied to your ass in any way. I don't want this brother coming after me like you are doing to him."

"Believe me, Portia, he won't be able to follow anyone when I am finished with his ugly ass."

"OK, I will try my best, and don't play with me, Shawn. I want my coat, and I may give you a little somethin' somethin' to remember me by if you can handle it," Portia said as she slowly spread her legs, tightening her well-fitted dress to accentuate every curve in her gorgeous body. "So, how do I identify this AJ person anyway?"

"You will know him because he is the only high, yellow-black dude on the wash line. He refuses to wear the company overalls, so he will be the guy in the white smock. He is there for another couple of hours if you can get over there today, Portia."

"What's the rush, Shawn, can't you give a girl a chance to get used to the idea and plan my gotcha game?"

"Portia, your gotcha game is always in high gear, so please go over there before he gets off, please. I am well overdue in paying this clown back for what he did."

"Okay, Shawn, I am on my way now, but I hope this guy is as easy as you seem to think." Portia walked toward her car with Shawn staring at the motion of her ocean. "Shawn, quit looking at my behind. It will cause you to be cross-eyed, my anxious friend. If this guy can be gotten, Portia will reel him in for sure big boy."

As Portia pulled into line at the car wash, many of the men were straining to get a look at who was driving the Beamer. As Portia approached being next in line, she slowly got out of the car with as much leg showing as possible, without exposing the obvious gold mine hidden beneath. She had on a short, sequined, tighter-than-hell dress, with all things matching to the nine. Even while looking like a million dollars, that fine tender roni in her pearl-white BMW 300 series did not sway me from my appointed rounds with Reba. Any other time, there would be no way that I wouldn't get those digits and add them to my player portfolio.

I know that I am a bad dude, but there was something wrong with this picture. She did everything but come over and udress in front of me, trying to get my attention. The girl was stacked, not hard to look at, with a booty like Faye's. It was obvious that she was well taken care of because of the diamonds on her hand and in her ears. I walked over to her and asked what particular service she wanted. Her response was "Full service, for my car and . . . me." This girl was too obvious. I had met forward women before, but for one who didn't know me from Adam's house cat, she was somewhat suspect.

<u>There was something about this girl that just wasn't right.</u> I didn't take the bait. I reached for her keys and found myself in a tug-of-war.

She was staring deeply into my eyes but held tightly to the keys. "Will I get my request or not?" I gave her an emphatic "Yes, I will take care of your car," and snatched the keys from her hand. A girl as well-kept as her seemed a bit out of place trying for a pickup at the car wash. This woman could call her shots at the best places in Chicago, so what was this all about? Old AJ didn't just fall off the cabbage truck. This felt like a setup. I kept my eyes on her while the car was being taken care of, and she did the same to me. I could feel her presence as I went about my duties.

When the car was wiped clean and sparkling like new money, I walked up to the hold area to let her know that the car was finished. She was busy talking on the cell phone. As I approached her, she walked out of range so that I couldn't hear her conversation.

Portia, seeming disappointed in her ability to draw AJ'S interest, immediately called Shawn expressing her frustration. "Shawn, this guy is either gay, or a cold fish. I have never had a man not ask for my number when I all but offered him the works. What do you want me to do?"

Porthia, you are a pro girl, you know how to handle a weak kneeded chump like him, "Try sliding him your number and see if he takes it. If he takes it, he has fallen for the bait. If he doesn't, we are back at square one."

As she walked back toward me, she took a card from her purse. "Mr. ah, ah . . . I didn't catch your name."

"That's because I didn't give it. Who is asking anyway?" Without any sign of being friendly, I said, "My name is AJ, and I just wanted to tell you that your car is ready."

"Well, that's more like it, Mr. AJ. My name is Portia, and it's indeed a pleasure to meet you. What about the second part of my request?"

"Thanks but no thanks, though I am flattered, I have to get back to work, Portia. It was nice meeting you too."

"AJ, can't you give a girl a call sometime? I usually don't have to work this hard to get someone to call me." She reached out and grabbed my hand and placed her card in my palm. "I am not in the habit of giving out my number to anyone who has no intention of using it. Will you use it?"

I smiled and backed away, leaving Portia to wonder if I would or not. If she was on the up-and-up, I had the upper hand, and I would play it only if I chose to do so. I walked a few feet away and decided to look back. If she was still standing there looking disgusted, I had played the right card, but if she had turned to walk away, this had been more than just a visit to the car wash. I turned, and Portia was still standing there, looking as pissed as ever. A fine woman like that, it had to hurt to be given the cold shoulder but she was at the wrong place at the wrong time. Though I felt good by her reaction and I probably would follow up with a call later, I still couldn't get it out of my head that this was too easy. All of a sudden, I was being surrounded with opportunity and beautiful women.

Portia immediately got on the phone to Shawn to tell him how things went. "Shawn, what the hell did you do to me? Man, that guy is no pushover. He all but made me feel like a hooker trying to run a game. I did everything but screw him on the spot, and that cold fish threw water on my fire."

"Well, Portia, thanks for trying, and usually there is more than one way to skin a cat. If I can't get to him one way, I will find another. He has a fine little baby sister that is ready to be plucked."

"Wait, just hold on, Shawn. I know you are not talking about what I think you are talking about. That's sick, so keep me out of any more of your devious plans. I am out of here."

CHAPTER VIII

Reba's Return

After work, I hurried home and put on my houndstooth jacket, black pants, and black gators. I snapped on my kangoand placed an extra amount of love portion on my neck and the chest hair that was slightly showing above the unbuttoned black silk shirt. Man, I was so sharp that I cut myself three times before I got out of the flat. As I started to open the door on my way out, the phone rang again. Now what? I said to myself. Could it be Ashley taking one final shot at me, or was it Reba making sure I was still coming? I thought it best that I not take a chance and have to do more lying to cover my tracks. As I glanced down at the phone screen, I noticed it was from the hospital, and I knew without a doubt that it was Ashley.

My car was in the garage out back. I did not drive it to work most of the time because it was cheaper to take the bus, and I was pinching the hell out of pennies to make ends meet. My ride was a 2010 Mustang, not something a player like me would have, but dependable nonetheless. It was a red convertible with a sunroof, saddle interior, and a sound system to die for. If Reba did happen to want a ride, I was ready. I wasn't worried because I was just going there for a drink or two or three. I licked my fingers, ran them across the front of my cap, slid in the ride, and off I went.

As I got about three miles outside the city limits, the phone rang. Thinking it was Reba checking on my arrival time, I said, "What, you can't wait to see old AJ?" The voice on the other end said, "AJ, who are you saying that to? Did you change your mind? Are you on your way to get me?" Shit, its Ashley . . . Now what am I going to do? I had to think fast. "Hi, baby, just kidding. I knew it was you, but I was just playing. I am on my way to meet Ray-Ray and will be back later tonight. Have a good time at the event." I waited a minute to see if I had dodged the bullet. Not only did I not dodge the thing, it hit me square in the heart. "AJ, I told you not to play with me." Just as quickly as the words left her lips, she hung up. A few minutes later, the phone rang again, and it was a hospital number but not Ashley's number. Was it Ashley again, or someone else? I ignored the call this time and focused on Reba and what I hoped to be a great evening. If the call was important, they would leave a message, and I could get it later.

Each white stripe in the highway seemed to go by almost in slow motion as I wondered what Ashley meant in her comments. As I entered the city of Indy and made my way to the Marriott Hotel where Reba was staying, I couldn't help but notice the Benzes, BMWs, Aston Martins, and Jags coming in and out of the entry. I pulled up to the entry, and a bellman asked me if he could help me. Most of the time, they will ask you if you are checking in. I guess that was the first sign that I didn't belong.

As I entered the lobby, a major hesitation engulfed me as I stood among the who's who of blue blood society. I had called Reba to let her know that I was in the lobby, but that was ten minutes ago. I stared at my watch for a minute before looking up and seeing Reba coming toward me. She had a sleek, black dress that hugged her curves like a silk pillow case. She was accented with a string of black pearls that cost more than my car, my flat, and all of my other possessions two times over. I was certainly out of my league. I was so focused on the majestic figure coming in my direction and didn't notice the six-foot-four-inch-framed superman just behind her.

"AJ, it's so good to finally see you again. You look good, as usual. I want you to meet a good friend of mine, Roger, who accompanied me to the event tonight. Roger is one of the partners at the law firm that I work for." At that point, my eyes looked like the red-and-white rotating cylinders outside of most barbershops. Roger grabbed my hand and placed it in a vice-like grip that almost caused me to scream out like a little bitch.

"Pleased to meet you, Roger," I spurted out.

"Likewise, I am sure, AJ."

Roger finally released the torque of a grip on my hand and turned to Reba and said that he would let us visit and that he would be in the ballroom. He kissed her on the jaw and did a military turn and was gone. I was still staring at the hunk of a man, I have to admit.

"AJ, AJ . . . Are you all right? It's really good to see you, my old friend. I am so happy that you came. Are you happy to see me?"

"Well, yes, Reba, just a little dazed at how lovely you are. You know that you and old AJ are connected, girl."

"Thanks, AJ, let's go into the lounge and catch up." She reached over and kissed me on the cheek, and her breast rubbed my arm. It felt like a cloud. They were so soft that she must have sprinkled meat tenderizer or something on them every day for the last month.

Reba order a bottle of Barolo wine and asked if it was OK if we sit in a corner that had some privacy. I am not the classic wine drinker, but I was sharp enough to know that Barolo was top of the line. But what else could I expect—Boone's Farm ? I noticed that she pulled up very close to me as if she knew that I was nervous and she would have a calming effect on my nervous ass. Whatever she was trying to do, it was working.

"So tell me, Reba, what brings you to Nap Town?"

"Well, AJ, I am here for a conference of lawyers to discuss tort reform."

Tort who? I thought. I didn't want her to know that I didn't know what the heck she was talking about. I think she knew it too because she had this sort of sly grin as if to say I won't embarrass him, and believe me, I appreciated it.

"Tell me, AJ, what's going on in your life. It's been awhile. Are you seeing anyone?"

"Well, no, not really. I go out from time to time, but nothing serious. What about you, Reba?"

"Roger and I hang out, but I am not ready for the serious stuff. My practice comes first. Roger is cool and secure and has no hang-ups about what I do."

"Cool, Reba, he seems like a nice guy. I often think about you and wonder how you are doing. I see now that you are doing just fine." I gave her one of my patented smiles.

"AJ, I have to admit that I think of you also. We had a good friendship once, until your habits got in the way."

"No one knows that better than me, Reba, and I still kick myself for that."

"Well, that's water over the dam, AJ. Looking back is only for losers."

Just as things were getting interesting, the phone rang again, from the same number at the hospital.

"AJ, shouldn't you take it? It could be important."

"Nah, Reba, if it's important, they will leave a message. Now where were we before the interruption?"

"I am getting a little tipsy, AJ. Would you walk me to my room to freshen up a bit?"

It was the first time that I had ever been afraid of a woman, but that first time had come. She seemed so in control, and I felt out of place. As we got on the elevator, she grabbed my arm and pulled in close to me. I was hoping that she could not hear my heart beating like it was coming out of my chest. As we arrived at the eighteenth floor, she guided me to a corridor labeled Master Suites. We stopped in front of 1823, and she handed me the key and asked that I open the door for her. Once inside, the room opened up into a large living area with couches and chairs that were fit for a king. Reba was definitely a queen and deserved every inch of this glorious pad. I could see that there was a Jacuzzi bath and a shower with a head at each end of the shower stall, probably to accommodate Roger and her. Was this the same Reba who left Chicago? The innocence was definitely gone. She had left the Mormon look far behind, and I was enjoying every bit of it.

As I continued to look up and around as if I was standing in Times Square in New York, Reba appeared with nothing on but a G-string and a bra, and two glasses for the champagne that she had chilling in the bedroom. My heart was at cardiac arrest stage now, but I was just going to have to die because I was going with the flow. All I could think of, other than the voluptuous melons hanging off her chest, was what if Roger would come in and see us? Man, I would not stand a chance with that dude. He looked as if he could tackle Mike Tyson with ease.

Reba, sensing my hesitancy, came over to me and gently rubbed my member until it ached like a freshly pulled tooth. She put her tongue in my ear, and I was about to explode. She went to a switch on the wall, and with a flick, the lights dimmed and soft music from Luther Vandross filled all the empty space in the room with "A House Is Not a Home." She had me, and she knew it. I was just a pawn on her chessboard. She was making the moves, and there was nothing I could or wanted to do about it. Before I knew it, we were intertwined like a well-woven rope. I have never been to heaven, but this must be somewhere near it because I was seeing streets of gold and could have sworn that I saw angels.

Reba moaned so loud as she took my member and did things with it that would have caused Jerry Springer to turn a bright shade of red. She controlled the process like I was her bitch. Sweat was popping off my forehead like the raindrops that was pounding the windows from the storm that still raged outside. The friction from our rotating bodies gave off so much heat that I thought that the sprinklers would go off. It was hard hearing her sensuous moaning over mine. It seemed like only seconds had passed, but actually it had been close to forty-five minutes. As we lay there quietly, I couldn't help but ask, "Reba, what about Roger?"

"What about Roger?" she shot back.

"Well, I thought . . ."

"You think too much, AJ."

And once again, she started to thrust and shake on my member until she sucked me completely dry. I had never felt the loss of control as I had at that moment. We both ended up at the foot of the bed somehow, but who cared? I was in Reba heaven. Though she was not quite as skilled as Faye, she had the total package. Faye seemed overwhelmed by the lovemaking experience, but Reba seemed melancholic. It was as if it was just another roll in the hay for her. The Reba that I knew back in college was long gone, you can believe that.

We were lying there in the moment, smelling the soft aroma of some serious lovemaking, when I must have dozed off. I was awakened by the sounds of the streets below and the voice of other hotel guests moving in the halls. I glanced over Reba to the radio clock on the nightstand, and it said 6:00 a.m. I popped up, hoping that I was mistaken, but it was indeed the next morning. I had the best time of my entire life, but that life was in jeopardy when I returned to Chicago.

Reba heard my movement and turned to see me pacing the floor near the window. "What's up, AJ? You seem restless."

"Nah, Reba, I just was supposed to get back last night because I had promised a friend that I would come by and help him move into his new crib."

"AJ, some things never change. You couldn't lie well when we were together back in school, and you still don't. You are dating someone, and now you don't have an excuse for being away all night."

"Nah, Reba, you got it wrong. There is no one I have to answer to. You are trippin'."

Reba started to smile as if to say Yeah, right and turned back over.

"By the way, what happened to Roger . . . Was he not staying here with you?"

"You let me worry about Roger. Unlike you, I have my life in order, and Roger knows what time it is."

Boy, I must be a cheap novel because these chicks are reading me chapter and verse. "Yo, Reba, I gotta go now, but when can I see you again?"

"Why do you want to see me again, AJ? It seems that very little has changed since I last saw you. You are still not in control of your life."

"Listen, girl, last night was the bomb, and I want to see you again and soon."

"No, AJ, it was just sex. Good sex, I have to admit, but just sex. We both enjoyed the moment, so let's move on. Not once during our lovemaking did you say how you felt about me. I was really waiting for that. Please lock the door on the way out. Good seeing you again, AJ."

I had just had a lesson in total control, and my teacher had just burst my bubble. I thought that I had just completed the masterpiece of my career in lovemaking, and it was reduced to a one-night stand by the finest instructor this side of Chicago. I had just been raped by the master rapist and still had to face Ashley. Ashley was no slouch in bed, but she was an amateur compared to Reba and Faye. I sat in my car for what seemed like hours, just taking in what just happened. I knew that it would probably be the last time I would see Reba, but I could say that both Faye and Reba were in a class of their own. I headed back to Chi Town hoping that the ride back would give me some ideas of how to face Ash.

The storm had passed over now and things seemed calm, but what was in store for me when I get back to Chicago? It was a long ride back, thinking of how to smooth this over with Ashley. The mind is a terrible thing to waste, and my mind was spilling all over the car seat. I had no idea what to say to Ashley about my meeting with Ray-Ray. How could I have chosen seeing an old friend over taking Ash to this event that was important to her? She was the one always in my corner but also always the one at the bottom of my list. I kept stepping into a pile of cow dong and didn't have the sense to clean my shoes off.

I parked in the garage and sauntered up to the apartment. I usually get a call from Ashley on Saturday morning, so I checked the messages. The only message that I had was from Pookie. His message was that he had some important information for me. Pookie never calls me, so what was it now? I picked up the phone to dial.

"Pookie, what's up, dude?"

"AJ, man, you better cover your tail. I saw that same car that was at the car wash cruising the neighborhood today. It passed your crib at least three times, man, so you better watch your back."

Now I am really trippin' because this is too much of a coincidence. Why was this same car showing up at the car wash and now on my street?

I had a lot on my mind and wasn't thinking clearly. "Okay Pookie, good looking out. I don't know who would think I was important enough to worry about, but something is up. Thanks again for looking out for a brother, but I am sure it's just a coincidence. Man, I have been screwing up royally lately. I went to Indianapolis to see Reba, my old flame, and I didn't take Ash to an event at the hospital. I need to call her to smooth things over."

"All right, my male whore of a friend. These women are going to rip your balls off and feed them to you one at a time."

"Haha, my brother, I got this. Ash will come around, you will see."

As I hung up the phone, there was still no call from Ash. What was up with her? She had always been so predictable. I would have normally heard from her by now. Now it was getting late in the day, and still no call. Against my better judgment, I picked up the phone to call her, but there was no answer. I tried her cell phone, but with the same result. It was not like Ashley to not return my calls, so something wasn't right.

As I took off my clothes to relax a bit, I had forgotten to turn my phone back on. On the screen was another call from the hospital. As I opened my voicemail, my mother's voice was the first I heard. "AJ, where are you? Please, please call us as soon as possible. Chantal is in the hospital and is in critical condition. She was attacked on the way home from school. That's all I can say right now, but please call." My heart seemed to jump right out of my chest. I couldn't believe what I had just heard. Was I dreaming? When the initial shock wore off, I hurried to dress and headed for the hospital. Why couldn't I have answered the calls? While I was out chasing dreams with Reba, my little sister was lying in a hospital, holding on to life. If I had just taken one of the calls, I would have known about my little sister.

As I entered the emergency wing of the hospital and approached the information desk, a silver-headed nurse asked if she could help me.

"Yes, I am looking for the room of Chantal James who was admitted yesterday."

"Oh yes, she is in room 554. Are you a relative?"

"Yes, I am. I am her brother."

"Sir, I had to ask because only immediate family is allowed in her room at this time."

As I entered the elevator headed for the fifth floor, I couldn't help but feel that I had let my family down by not being here. What had happened to my little sister while I was out pleasuring myself? How selfish could I have been? I just didn't know, I didn't know.

As I got off of the elevator, my heart was beating as if it was going to jump out of my chest. The first person I saw was Aunt Doll, who stopped me before entering the room.

"What happened to Chantal, Aunt Doll?"

"We don't know yet, baby, but what we do know is that she was beaten pretty badly and sexually assaulted on her way home from school. Someone painted the word PAYBACK on her legs. The doctor said that she will be Okay but will take some time to heal psychologically from the rape."

Tears started to roll from my eyes as I slid down the wall to the floor. How could someone do that to Chantal, so young, so innocent? Could something that I had done in the past have caused this? Moms came out to the hall and just stared at me with a disgusted look on her face.

"AJ, where were you? We were trying to get you all night. Where were you?"

"Moms, please forgive me. I didn't know, and I had my phone off because I had been getting so many calls that I didn't want to take. I had agreed to meet an old friend in Indy for a few drinks. I am sorry, Moms! Do they have any idea who did this?"

"No, not yet. The only thing that they know is someone observed a red Mustang with large tires speeding away from the area where Chantal was found. The driver was wearing a hoodie, so no one was able to get a clear look at him. There were two others in the car. Sounds like some of the gangbangers, but no one knows for sure. They were able to get some faint prints from her purse and some skin where she was able to scratch the attacker. Maybe the cops will be able to get an ID from that."

My mind immediately went to the red Mustang similar to mine that pulled away just as I was leaving the car wash and how Shawn had threatened to get even because of Faye. But Shawn drove a silver Lexus, not a Mustang.

I would find who did this to my little sister if it was the last thing that I did, you can bet on that. Pookie had also warned me about someone who might have something against me. I could not live with myself if I caused this to happen to Chantal.

I finally mustered up enough nerve to go in to see Chantal. I was horrified to see what had been done to that pretty little girl, my sister, my special blessing from God. Her face was swollen, scratches were on her arms and neck, and IV tubes were running in her arms and nose. I couldn't help but turn away and, in an instant, started to punch the wall over and over until blood flowed from both hands. Suddenly, I felt strong hands grab my shoulder and hug me tightly. It was my pops. I couldn't remember the last time that he showed any emotion toward me or told me he loved me, but it was better late than never. "AJ, it's all right, son, it's all right. We will find who did this to our baby."

I pulled away slightly and looked in Pops' eyes, and for the first time, I believed him. There was fire in his eyes that I had never seen before. "Pops, no doubt, we will find the sick sucker who did this, or we will die trying."

Just then, a slight noise came from Chantal. She was calling my name in a hushed voice. I quickly rushed to her bedside and leaned over to see if I could make out what she was saying. The only thing I could hear was the word white. Was she trying to tell me that it was a white boy who did this? Before I could ask her to repeat it, her eyes closed, and she was back into a deep sleep from the anesthesia.

"AJ, could you hear what she was saying?" said Aunt Doll.

"No, I couldn't make it out. Maybe she will try again when she wakes up." I didn't want the family to know what Chantal had said, because if I found out that it was Shawn who had violated my little sister, I would terminate his ass and wouldn't think twice about it.

With all of Pookie's connections to the streets, there should be someone who could give us an idea of what happened to Chantal. Guys who do this type of thing eventually want to share it with someone, and I hoped he did. At this point, nothing mattered other than finding out who did this. I was feeling guilty for not being here for Chantal, for not being here when the family needed me.

I left the hospital in a daze. I was determined to spend the time and money tracking down this lowlife who hurt Chantal. I had rediscovered my pops but came close to losing my sister. Could Shawn be behind this, or could he have hired someone else to commit the crime? After all, he had threatened to get even with me, and the word PAYBACK written on Chantal's legs seemed to indicate that her attacker was looking for revenge, but on whom? Chantal was loved by all who knew her in the neighborhood.

After leaving the hospital, I rode around for what seemed like two hours, looking for the red Mustang before returning to my crib for some much-needed rest. I couldn't get the image of Chantal lying cut and bruised in that hospital bed out of my mind. It was a sleepless night, and I woke up constantly, feeling helpless. Revenge was the order of the day, and I would not rest until I had it. Could this have just been a random attack and Chantal was just in the wrong place at the wrong time?

Later that evening, I got a call from Moms asking that I come over to meet with the detectives who thought that they might have a lead. I hurried to moms's apartment in hopes that there was enough to burn the son of a mother who did this to Chantal.

As I walked into the apartment, moms introduced me to Detective Hathaway of the Chicago PD. "Detective, this is our son, AJ. We wanted him here to hear what evidence you have."

"Good to meet you, son. We were fortunate that we were able to get some good tissue samples and a print from the crime scene thanks to your daughter's actions. Evidently, in her attempt to fight them off, she was able to get them to grab her purse, probably while she was hitting them. She was also able to scratch one of them during the attack. The print is one of a person by the name of Alex Brower. There is no criminal record on this guy, but he was involved somehow. Do either of you know of anyone by that name?" Mom and Pops said no, and they looked at me.

I shook my head, but in the back of my mind, I knew that Shawn's friend from the hotel was named Alex. "Detective, what about the DNA from the skin sample?"

"Well, son, another fortunate result, though it was someone else that had no past criminal record. It was from a guy named Shawn Samuels. We check all of the gang activity, and they are not listed gang members."

When I heard Shawn's name, my heart dropped. I said to myself, I knew it, I knew it, and I knew it. I was hoping that the detective didn't see me clenching my teeth and fist as Shawn's name was mentioned.

"Well, folks, we have our detectives out on the street looking for these thugs, and we hope to have them real soon."

I whispered under my breath, "I hope not, if I get to them first."

Mama said, "Thanks, detective, for all that has been done to fine these animals."

"You are welcome, Mrs. James. We will make sure that they don't do this to some other person."

I returned to my apartment to decide my next move. It was Shawn who had raped my little sister, and he would pay dearly for that. It was Sunday morning and still no word from Ashley. My macho would not let me call her again. There was still a slight drizzle outside, and I had no desire to go out, if it weren't for the fact I did not having anything in the fridge. As I settled to watch a little TV, Pookie called and wanted me to meet him at Joe's Crab Shack. Maybe he had heard about what happened to Chantal. I didn't think to ask him while on the phone. He sounded rushed, so I threw on a pair of jeans, a sweatshirt, and my pullover sweater, and rushed to meet Pookie, not just to hear him ramble on about nothing but because Joe had some of the best barbeque ribs on this side of town. I had decided not to mention what I knew about the attack to anyone until I had decided my next move.

As I rolled up to the parking lot, Pookie was waving his arms frantically for me to stop. "AJ, are you ready for this?"

"Ready for what? Are you going to tell me who hurt my little sister?"

"Your little sister . . . you mean someone hurt Chantal?"

"Yes, I thought you knew. When I find out who did this, there is not enough real estate on earth to hide the dude. Man, someone followed her from school and beat and raped her something awful."

"That's really sick, and I will ask around to see if anyone heard or saw anything."

"I was hoping you would say that, Pookie, you are my boy."

"AJ, that's the least I can do, and if I find the sucker before you do, his ass is grass and I am the lawnmower."

"Nah, Pookie, if you find him, I need to know because I have a score to settle. No one does that to my little princess and live to tell about it. I swear, I will cut his balls off and push them down his throat. Now, Pookie, what was it you got me down here to tell me?"

"This doesn't seem important now, AJ, but what I called you down here for is that Ashley is in the Shack with another dude. I didn't want you to freak out over the phone."

"No big deal, Pookie, it's probably one of the dweebs that she works with."

"I don't think so, my brother with blinders on, they are too cozy to be just working buddies."

As I entered the restaurant, I could see Ashley sitting with her back to me, and the guy she was with was draped all over her. As I approached the table where they were sitting, I wondered how she would react once she recognized me. I called out, "Ash, is that you?"

"Oh, hi, AJ, a little surprised to see you here."

"That I am sure of, Ashley, and aren't you going to introduce me to your friend?"

"I hadn't planned to, but since you asked. Raphael, this is AJ. AJ, this is Raphael, and in case you are wondering, AJ, he knows all about you." Though I had accused her of being surprised to see me, she really didn't seem surprised at all. In fact, she acted as if she didn't give a damn whether I saw her or not. I may have pushed Ash over the line this time. I wanted my cake and eat it too, but it seems that Ash had closed the dessert line.

"Why haven't I heard from you, Ash? We were going to get something to eat yesterday. What's up?"

"Spare me the drama, AJ, you don't have time for me, and I don't have time for your games. The days are over that I sit around and wait for you to get around to me. I am moving on. And by the way, I hope you had a good time with your friend in Indy."

Ash said it like she knew why I was in Indy. Did she know that I was with Reba and is just playing me? It was hard for me to be upset after spending the night with Reba, so I put on my mack face and played it off as if it was nothing. "Yo, Raphael, good meeting you, dude. You guys have a nice day, and take care of Ash. She is a good woman." I gave Ash a final look and walked toward the exit. If she wanted a hotdog over this T-bone steak, then it's her call. I have to admit that it pissed me off to see her sitting there with that dweeb draped around her.

Pookie was waiting outside, staying away from what he thought would be fireworks. "What's up, man, you OK?"

"Yeah, man, I'm cool. She is pissed at me for not taking her to a work function this weekend, so she decided to step out on me, but I'm cool."

As I returned to my apartment, I could hear the phone ringing as I entered the door. "Hello."

"Hello, AJ, I didn't want us to end that way, so I wanted to call and tell you that I couldn't do this anymore. I was not your priority, and it was becoming painfully obvious. I received a call from someone telling me that you were in Indy to meet an old girlfriend. Is that true, AJ? I just need to know the truth."

"Ash, I didn't want to hurt you, but my old friend was in Indy for a conference and agreed to meet me for a drink. She is just a friend, and we got a little carried away with the celebrating. I was in no condition to drive home, so I got a room for the night, and I should have told you."

"AJ, you see what I mean about priorities. Whoever she is, she was your priority and not me. I need someone in my life that I can trust, and I can't trust you anymore. It's best that we give each other some space, and I wanted to tell you that. Good-bye, AJ."

As we hung up the phone, I realized how much of a mess my life was, and now it had spilled over into my relationships. Ash had been good to me, and I again had blown yet another relationship because of my bush league actions. As much as I cared at one time about Reba, it was Ashley that had stood by me, and I had let her down. I was determined to make it up to Ash in some way; I owe her that much even if she never takes me back. I tried sending flowers, candy, and calls to Ash after that, and she never responded.

For the next couple of weeks, I drove around looking for Shawn and his posse. They were nowhere to be found. Maybe they had left town, trying to wait until the current situation clears. They were probably unaware that they were wanted by the Chicago PD and now me. From that point, it was off to work and back home. I didn't answer the phone or hang out in the normal places. I just wanted to get my head straight and try and refocus my life. Seeing Reba and how well she has done made me realize that life is more than good sex and a few dollars in your pocket. From this point on, I would dedicate my time to finding Shawn and Alex and somehow figure out a way to get back in ash's good grace.

It was 8:00 p.m. and Pookie had been snooping around for weeks, trying to find a lead. I didn't want to let him know that I knew who did this and their asses were mine. I really didn't want to get him involved in what I was going to do to those suckers. Pookie was known to be a bloodhound, so we got the break that we had been hoping for.

While shooting pool at the pool hall on the corner of Hillside and Baker, Pookie overheard a conversation between two white guys who were sitting at the bar and who obviously had overindulged in mixing beer and alcohol. One guy was tall and well-built, and the other was short and stocky. The taller, more athletically built guy was bragging about something he had done in retaliation for someone who had wronged him. He went on to say how he had hit the guy's sister in retaliation and was laughing hysterically about it. Pookie got on the phone to call me.

"AJ, we may have hit pay dirt. I am at a little sleazy bar on Hillside and Baker. I overheard this conversation that I am sure you will be interested in. These two white guys were talking about hitting some dude's sister in retaliation for something. One dude was named Alex, and the other was that dude that you went to school with named Shawn. I have seen you guys talking a time or two."

"Pookie, are you sure? Are you sure what you heard?"

"AJ, get your ass down here right now before they leave."

Was this the break that I have been looking for? Shawn had violated Chantal and would not live to see tomorrow if I could help it. I had a Saturday night special in my car that just may come in handy. I got dressed and headed to meet Pookie.

After arriving at the bar, I walked into the side entry so that anyone sitting at the bar could not see me. I spotted Pookie sitting in a booth directly across from where four men and a woman were sitting at the bar. Two of the men were definitely Shawn and Alex. After a few minutes had passed, Alex stood up to leave, but Shawn remained. They exchanged farewells and parted ways.

"Pookie, are you absolutely sure what you heard? Because if you are, these guys won't leave here alive."

"Wait, AJ. What are you talking about, man? You better call the cops. I will tell them what I heard."

"Pookie, it would be your word against their word, and I don't hold a lot of hope that they will believe you over a white boy. It doesn't matter anyway because the cops already know that these dudes did Chantal and are looking for them too. Here is what I want you to do. I want you to go over to the bar and strike up a conversation with Shawn while I take care of his buddy that just left. Tell him that you overheard his conversation and that you know he was talking about me because my sister was attacked and is in the hospital. Can you do that, Pookie? His behavior after hearing that someone knows will be a telling fact. If he bites on that, then we got the sucker."

While Pookie was preparing to approach Shawn, I hurried to catch Alex. I followed him a ways from the bar where he had parked his car on a dark street next to a vacant lot. As he opened the door, I shouted out, "Yo, Alex, what's up, my white brother?"

"Is that you, AJ? What are you doing around here, man?"

"Just so happens I am looking for you, my perverted friend."

"Looking for me for what?"

"My little sister wanted me to say hello."

It was obvious that he knew now why I was there and was obviously nervous because he dropped his keys. As he bent down to pick them up, I hit him with the butt end of the pistol. As he laid there begging me to not shoot him, he started to talk. "AJ, please, don't shoot me. It was Shawn who raped your sister. I had nothing to do with it."

"Yeah, but you were there and did nothing to stop it."

"Yes, I was there, but what could I do? You know how Shawn is, man."

"That's too bad, Alex, because you are guilty for being his friend, and it was your other buddy's skin under my little sister's fingernails."

As I loaded a round in the chamber, he held his hand up to cover his face. I screwed on a silencer so as to not have the sound detected. "AJ, man, I'm sorry! I didn't want him to hurt anyonePlease, man, I didn't do nothing."

"Yes, Alex, you are sorry, and I am sorry for what I am about to do . . . This is for Chantal"— pop, pop—"and this one is for being a dumb coward." Pop, pop.

It was easier than I thought. I could only think of Chantal and not the lifeless body lying crumpled on the street at my feet. Luckily, the streets were deserted, and I was hoping that no one observed what I had just done. I grabbed him by his feet and dragged him into some high brush in the adjacent vacant lot and covered him with cardboard and trash. As I reentered the bar from a side door and waited in the shadows, I could clearly hear the conversation between Pookie and Shawn.

Pookie was sitting to the right of Shawn. Shawn glanced over at Pookie and without hesitation said, "What's up man, I have noticed you looking at us. So what's up?"

", I overheard you and your friend talking about getting revenge for something that someone had done to you. I just happen to know that a guy named AJ was telling people about his sister being raped and beaten. It's not my business, but I have never liked that dude and though I feel sorry for his sister, he got what was coming to him. I have been looking forward to getting back at that guy since he clipped me for some money when we were in jail, said Pookie." "See, that's what I am talking about, you know that punk too" He really makes my blood boil."

Shawn was beginning to feel more comfortable with Pookie and started to loosen up and talk. "Yea, man" said Pookie, "you have nothing to worry about because your debt has been paid. That young, tender thing was easy pickings, and now part of my revenge is complete, said Shawn." With a big smile and a wink, Shawn got up to leave, paid his tab, and started out the front entrance. Pookie gave me the thumbs-up, and left through the side door. I felt like cold cocking the son of a mother right there, knowing now what he had done to Chantal.

Pookie hurried out to find me holding a gun to Shawn's head. "I finally got your ass, Shawn. Now tell me what you were bragging about in the bar."

"What the hell are you talking about, AJ?"

At that point, Pookie rounded the corner to the alley where I was holding Shawn. "AJ, I overheard that punk laughing about what he did to Chantal, and he admitted it to me at the bar."

Shawn laughingly said, "It's my word against yours, and who do you think the cops will believe?"

"Unfortunately for you, you are so right, Shawn, and that is why this has to end right here, right now." I didn't want to tell him that the cops knew that he was a part of the rape of my sister. If the cops got to him first, he may get off too easily, and I can't have that.

"You are a big man with that gun in your hand, AJ," said Shawn.

"Well, this is for Chantal." The first shot rang out, striking Shawn in the right upper thigh. A second shot hit him in the left lower leg, the third in the shoulder, and the fourth in the chest. It was indeed my intention to end it there. As I raised the gun for the final time and pointed it at Shawn's head, police sirens pierced the night air. Pookie and I, realizing the gravity of the situation, took off toward the other end of the ally. I told Pookie to go alone because they may be looking for two of us.

As Pookie and I arrived back at the crib, I realized that unless Shawn had died, we would get a visit from the police very soon. Pookie was in better shape as far as the cops were concerned because Shawn never knew his name

Several days passed and no cops came to my door. Had Shawn died? Was he in a coma? The phone rang, and I was afraid to answer. It rang a second and third time, and finally I had to answer. It was Pookie.

"AJ, I heard that that guy Shawn was going to survive and that he was not talking to anyone including the cops. What's that about? Why would he protect you after what you did?"

"I don't know, Pookie, I have to be prepared for anything."

At that point, a knock was at the door. As I looked through the peephole, I saw it was Pops. He had never set foot in my place, so what was this about? I opened the door and welcomed him in.

"AJ, any luck in finding out who violated Chantal?"

"Pops, the less you know about this, the better. If they come looking for me, you are still around to protect the family. It wouldn't do to have us both in jail. Last night, I caught up with the guy that abused Chantal and I shot him four times. Before I had the chance to finish the job, the cops came, and I ran before they saw me. The dude is still alive, and why he hasn't ratted me out, I don't know. Pops, I wanted him to suffer like Chantal did. I wanted to punish him before ending his life."

"Well, son, I'm glad that you didn't, because attempted murder is no comparison to murder. He is still alive, and I too have mixed feelings about that. I have a detective friend down at the courthouse that I will talk to on your behalf. He will understand that it was because of the abuse to your sister that you did what you did. Thanks, son. It won't fix what happened to Chantal, but to know that he has suffered as a result of what he did gives me some comfort."

Pops was a man of his word, and after sharing what Pookie had overheard between Shawn and Alex, plus the evidence to Pops's detective friend, I was released and placed on two-year probation. Shawn, after confessing to the rape, was given seven years with early release for good behavior. That was still too good for what he did, and I would not forget it.

Alex's body was found sometime later and assumed to be a victim of the surrounding drug wars. There had been many unsolved murders in that area, so the cops just added another. I was feeling a lot of grief for taking a life, and I was sure that it would catch up to me later. The gun that I used had been deposited in the river and, to that point, had not been found.

A few weeks had passed, and my life was in shambles. I had not heard from Ashley or Reba, so I decided to finally test my assumption on Portia.

"Hello, Portia, it's AJ from the car wash, remember?"

"Oh yes, AJ . . ." There was a long pause. "What's up?"

"I thought that maybe we could have a burger or something to get to know each other. I have to admit, I need a friend right about now."

"Well, AJ, I don't know."

"Please, Portia, I just need a little female companionship, and it's straight on the up and up."

Another pause from Portia before she said, "OK, AJ, maybe coffee and a sandwich would work. What about the little coffee shop on King Drive near the old Howard Theater? I will meet you there around 5:00 p.m."

I arrived at the coffee shop a little early so that I could get a good seat and observe Portia when she entered. I am still a little unsettled by how we met.

Portia arrived wearing a short leather skirt hugging every curve and inch of her gorgeous body. I stood to greet her, and we both slid into the tight booth area.

"Hi, AJ, it's good to finally meet you. I thought you had pitched my number the same evening that we met. You must understand why I feel that way after giving a girl the cold shoulder as you did."

"Portia, it was just the wrong time and the wrong place. I was going through a lot then, and I had no room for anything or anyone at that point. I was a little curious as to why you gave a brother that kind of attention."

"What you will find out about me, Mr. AJ, is that I am not shy when I see something I want."

Portia ordered a decaffeinated coffee and a bagel while I had a fully loaded cup of high-octane coffee because I needed the caffeine. I topped it off with a piece of apple pie. "So, Portia, tell me about yourself. Why did you give this brother so much play at the car wash a few months back?"

"Well, AJ, like you needed a friend, I thought you were a nice guy and not hard to look at. What about you?"

"Well, Portia, I don't know if you read about it in the papers, but my baby sister was molested and severely beaten by a guy who was trying to get revenge because I dated his girl. He followed her home from school and beat and molested her. She was just recently released from the hospital. I shot the dude four times but did not kill him, though I would have if the cops had not arrived. I am not a violent person, but I see red if someone messes with my family. His name was Shawn."

As soon as I said his name, Portia almost choked on her coffee, and her beautiful mahogany skin turned pale.

"Are you OK, Portia?"

"Yes, I am OK, just drinking a little too fast. What did this guy Shawn look like, AJ?"

"He was just a buff white boy who loves black women."

Portia acted like she had seen a ghost. All of a sudden, she was ready to leave. "AJ, sorry for having to cut our visit short, but I am not feeling well. Maybe we can do this another time."

"OK, Portia, I'm sorry that you are not feeling well. Please call me if you want to continue our conversation."

Portia left in a hurry. Her reaction really was suspicious. Did she know Shawn? Was it more than coincidental that we met at the car wash just prior to Chantal's rape? Had Shawn put her up to meeting me or trying to set me up? You could bet that this was not over. As long as Shawn is alive, my life would be unsettled.

As Portia left the café, she reflected on what had just happened. Did I hear what I thought I had heard? Did Shawn really rape that little girl and try to use me to get even with AJ? I have to know for sure if Shawn did what AJ seems to think he did. Portia dialed Shawn's number and found it had been disconnected. She tried the hospital, and sure enough, he had been treated for gunshot wounds and had been released in the custody of the police. That dirtbag tried to use me to do his dirty work. I hope he rots in hell.

I made my way through traffic to the hospital to see Chantal and to see if she can clearly tell me what happened. When I arrived at her room, she was sitting up in the bed, staring out of the window. She had lost her innocence, and her life was changed forever. "Chantal . . . Chantal," I called out. Chantal never shifted her focus from the window. Tears came to my eyes because I could see the damage, the hurt, the embarrassment that she would have to deal with at such a young age. Death was too good for Shawn; he had to suffer the way that Chantal has.

I searched around and found that Shawn had been placed at the Metropolitan Correctional Center where I had taken up residency for a short period. I still had a few connections inside the walls. The whole while I was in there, I stayed close to the wall to protect my backside from the horny pissants who had not seen a woman for quite a while. When the hardcore alpha males set their sights on me, I was given a pass because of a monster of a man they called Red Brown. Red saw me as his little brother and looked out for me while I served my time. This dude had arms like tree trunks, tattoos from head to toe, a temper that frightened even the guards, and a set of eyes that sat back in his head like he had been drinking cough syrup all of his life. Back on the block, that cough syrup screwed up many badass dudes who thought they could handle it. When Big Red spoke, even E. F. Hutton listened. The man had a soft side until he was crossed. You would rather walk through hell with kerosene s drawers on rather than screw with Red.

I waited a few days for Shawn to settle down in his new digs before letting him know that I had not gone away. Visiting hours were from 3:00 p.m. until 6:00 p.m., so on the following Monday, I made it a point to be there to visit Red Brown, a drug dealer and bouncer who was serving time for stabbing a restaurant worker twelve times for spilling water on his suit. Red had been in and out of prison for petty theft many times before. As we all waited in the room with picnic tables scattered all over this large, open area, the prisoners were allowed to enter the area one at a time to be greeted by their visitors and take a seat at the table. As Shawn entered the room, I was standing near the entryway, and our eyes met.

Shawn immediately moved in my direction and was subdued by the guards. "You will pay for what you did to me, and you can bet on that, AJ."

"And you will pay for what you did to my little sister, you frickin' pervert."

At that point, a shadow came over the room when Red Brown came into the area to meet me. He had overheard part of the conversation.

"AJ, what's cooking, my little brother?"

"Red, that son of a mother standing over there raped my little sister."

Red snapped his head around in the direction of Shawn. "This piece of shit raped little Chantal? Oh, hell no, hell to the no." Red's eyes turned bloodshot, and sweat started to pour from underneath his toboggan cap like rain on a windowpane. Red pointed at Shawn and slowly walked away. "Good seeing you, AJ . . . I got it" was all he said as he was escorted by the guards back through the corridor. Shawn, realizing that he now could have an inside problem, slowly moved to a corner of the room and took a seat at a table, keeping his eyes on me. As I turned to leave, I wondered who would visit this loser. I waited another thirty minutes, and just as I started to leave, into the center of the room walked none other than Portia.

My intuition was right—she did know him, and her reaction at the coffee shop gave her away. As I watched their interaction, I could see an argument starting. Shawn reached for Portia's arm, and she pulled away. I could tell it was a heated exchange.

I stood inside of the door so that I could be seen by both. Shawn pointed in my direction, and Portia put her hands to her mouth and hurried to the door to leave. With a big smile on my face, I placed my finger to my throat in a cutting motion as he had once done, then pointed my finger in a shooting motion as if to say I got you now, you scumbag. I knew that Red Brown would take care of business.

I later got the word that Shawn had been sexually abused over and over by Red's boys and was a broken man. The last I heard of him was that he was living in some halfway house across town and surviving the best he could. What a comedown from the glory days of big money and hot black women. He was seen around town from time to time but was a shell of the man that he was. Chantal, with the help of therapy and much love from my family, made significant progress and was back in school.

I saw Portia once after that, and she broke down and cried. She did everything that she could to convince me that even though she knew Shawn, she had nothing to do with his sleazy plan to hurt Chantal. Portia turned out to be one of my best confidants and friends, and she had my back no matter what. No, I didn't hit it because I didn't feel that way about her, but she was one fine specimen of a woman.

Ashley had dropped her new play toy and had tried several times to rekindle our relationship. Though I had to spend some time revisiting Faye and her sexual ways and even made a few trips to visit Reba, I knew that Ashley was the one I could depend on. The thing I most liked about Ash was that she liked me for me, while the others were just about the sex thing.

I spent a lot of time working and reflecting on my life, my relationship, and my family from that point. Taking Ash out for a nice night on the town was really nice. I finally realized that doing special things for her and going places with her showed her how important she was to me and how special our relationship was. I was finally satisfied just being with her. Faye had her new life as a designer, Reba was a big-time prosecutor in New York City, and after all these years, I was still afraid of the dark.

There was one thing about Chicago summers: if you waited long enough, another one of those electric storms would come through the area. The weather report had said that the storm was twenty-four hours away, but boy, did they miss this one. As the clouds rolled in, lightning illuminated the night as if it were midday. I glanced at the clock on the stove, and it was blinking on and off from the storm. I lay down to rest for a few minutes, which ended up being a couple of hours. I was exhausted, and the last couple of months' activities were finally catching up to me.

On this dark and stormy evening, as the wind played a tune as it whistled between the buildings, the rain came down in sheets while the larger-than-normal drops banged against the windowpane like gunshots. I stood looking out over the sparsely lit streets of my neighborhood, still trying to understand the strange feeling that had dominated my mind since leaving work. I couldn't help but wonder just what was going on in the allies and corridors of the shanty houses bordering the streets at the corner of Fifteenth and Broadway. In fact, just looking at the rain glistening off the concrete and seeing the yellow glow of the lights from the apartments along the street sort of gave the old place a feeling of peace, and for that fleeting moment, it was my own little heaven.

I pressed my nose against the windowpane, and the warmth of my breath caused a dreary fog on the surface. My mind revisited the beatdown that Shawn had given me years before, the steamy and exhausting sex episodes with Faye and Reba, the difficult times with Ashley, and the friendship with Portia. I thought about the sacrifices that my parents had made for me and the terrible thing that had happened to Chantal. My life had been a series of mis-steps and my focus had been on the wrong things. As tears welled in my eyes, a single drop broke away from the rest, headed down my cheek, and landed in my hand.

I raised my head and focused on the street below. I could see a small dog running for cover to get out of the drenching downpour while other dogs braved the elements to find a morsel of food from the garbage cans on the curb to satisfy their extraordinary hunger. I could identify with them because the hunger pains were beginning to hit me as well. A police car with its siren blasting headed for another forgettable or unforgettable circumstance. Whenever I heard that sound, I breathed a sigh of relief that they were not coming for old AJ this time. I had spent more than my fair share of time in the back of those police cars, looking through the chicken wire barrier that separated the pigs from the innocent people like me who were accosted and carried to jail for simply WWB (walking while black).

As I glanced over the bars that covered the windows, I could not help but wonder what it would be like to, like the TV program *I Dream of Jeannie*, just blink my eyes, wiggle my nose, cross my arms and be transferred instantly to another place and time, away from the dark streets with broken streetlights, away from the constant gunfire of both police and gang warfare, away from the rooms with barely enough heat to keep us warm during these hard Chicago winters, away from the absentee dad and cocaine-addicted mom, away from the crying of my little sister because she was hungry, away from the roach-filled bedrooms and fridge with no food. Daydreaming was part of my pastime because it gave me hope, and it was all that I had to hold on to.

As I glanced in another direction, toward condemned buildings where junkies and prostitutes usually handled their entrepreneur activities on the street, I couldn't help but notice the eerie silence on this night. This was indeed unusual for this street where something was always going down, whether good or bad. Just as I turned to walk away and go back into the boredom of the flat, which reminded me of Fred Sanford's junkyard, a quick final look across the street revealed a shadowy figure appear from the alley, with a red-and-white Chicago Bulls throwback jersey and a rain-soaked New York Yankee ball cap pulled down slightly over his face, revealing large, bulging eyes and a narrow face that was engulfed in long, unkempt dreadlocks. He had both hands in his pocket as if he were on a mission. As I turned back to the window, I strained my eyes to try and focus on him, to see if I recognized this lone figure piercing the silent moonlit street below. He came closer and closer, giving me a good vantage point of his movement, but I still couldn't see his face. The hood and the cap were perfect covers to protect his identity.

Just as quickly as he stepped upon the curb on my side of the street, our eyes met, and in the blink of an eye, he removed his right hand from his pocket and I heard a pop, pop, pop. The glass where I was standing by shattered into pieces, and there I stood, looking down at a lifeless body lying at my feet. A warm feeling came over me as I viewed the wet, glass-covered linoleum floor beneath my feet where the body lay drenched in blood. The fallen figure seemed so quietly familiar, stretched out on the barren floor of my apartment. It took me only a moment to realize that the figure lying cold and still on my floor with his eyes seemingly locked on mine . . . was me. Shawn had gotten his revenge.

Snap out of it, and let's get back to reality. No, my brothers and sisters, this is not intended to be a murder mystery or a fictional novel but instead the reality of scenes played out in many of our cities across this land of plenty. It's what seems to have become the rule versus the exception for both innocent and noninnocent participants in the war for life.

I know, I know that I have just whetted your appetite for a murder-and-mayhem novel of greater length. You had prepared yourself for the reading with your glass of milk and wine, cheese and crackers. Not so fast. I really need your undivided attention on how young men like AJ could reverse the results of that short story. How do we transform his hope to an eventual reality?

I wanted to draw your attention to how young men can keep themselves out of situations like this character did. AJ was not able to find his way to the light switch. He was unable to make the ultimate decision to change his destructive direction. At some point in all of our lives, we get to the crossroads like AJ did, and sometimes we make the wrong decision. All wrong decisions do not take you to a dark place like AJ put himself in. The key here is to learn from your mistakes and not repeat them.

My intent here is to show that there may be a dark side to any of us, and circumstances like the abuse of young Chantal could be the trigger point as it was for AJ, who was not the type of young man who had experienced a life of murder. He made some bad decisions that followed him and eventually led to his death. There are a lot more AJs out there, and I hope this short novel will show how staying close to family, getting a good education, and respecting women are the right tools for the toolkit.

"Am I my brother's keeper?" is a question that should be answered by each of us, as brothers, men, husbands, fathers, and concerned citizens. What intrigues me about that is, unlike other cultures, we black men have gone through so many phases and challenges to our manhood. Luckily, many of us have not met the fate that our friend AJ did, though still so many have.

From the early days of slavery, when we black men were used like animals to breed, many were stripped of their dignity on the auction block, taken away from their families, and deposited on plantations miles from their children and wives. Others were beheaded, hanged, and castrated, and as a result, men of color have had a difficult time reestablishing our rightful place as heads of our families. We have had to muster up all of the testosterone and courage to move from the victim to the victor. These acts of crime—yes, I said crime—left undeniable scars on our image as leaders of our families, our communities, and most of all our self-esteem.

Anytime there is a deep cut in the skin, a resulting scar appears that is a constant reminder of the events that created that cut. Once anything is damaged, it is much more difficult to return its original form. A broken arm, a damaged heart, your car after an accident, and a relationship after a betrayal of trust—all are forever damaged no matter how hard you try to fix them. They may look the same on the surface, but underneath, there are scars reminding you of the damage. In addition to these scars are life's little constant reminders that the damage happened in the first place. It's like we are constantly looking over our shoulders because it's hard for us to trust anyone or anything.

These atrocities even sometimes cause our black women to question whether we are capable of leading because of the daze and depression that the scars caused. If we lose the trust of our mothers, daughters, and wives, it's like losing our manhood. It cuts deeply into the male ego and survival mentality. Without hope, we can't survive.

There is always some writing or poem that sums up your subject in a way that really brings the point home about how we live our lives, and here is such an article. It's called "Mayonnaise Jar and Two Beers." I could not find the author of this piece of work, but the credit goes to him or her. It goes like this:

A professor stood before his philosophy class and had some items in front of him. When the class began, he wordlessly picked up a very large and empty mayonnaise jar and proceeded to fill it with golf balls. He then asked the class if the jar was full, and they agreed that it was. The professor then picked up a box of pebbles and poured them into the open jar. He shook the jar lightly, and the pebbles rolled into the open area between the golf balls. Then he asked the students again if the jar was full, and they again agreed that it was. The professor next picked up a box of sand and poured it into the jar. Of course, the sand filled up everything else. He asked once more if the jar was full and the students responded with a unanimous "yes." The professor then produced two beers from under the table and poured the contents into the jar, effectively filling the empty space between the sand. The students laughed.

"Now," said the professor as the laughter subsided, "I want you to recognize that this jar represents your life. The golf balls are the important things—your family, your children, your health, your friends, and your favorite passion—and if everything else was lost and only they remained, your life would still be full. The pebbles are the other things that matter, like your job, your house, and your car. The sand is everything else—the small stuff.

"If you had placed the sand in the jar first," he continued, "there would be no room for the pebbles or the golf balls. The same goes for life. If you spend all of your time and energy on the small stuff, you will not have room for the things that are important to you. Pay attention to the things that are critical to your happiness. Spend time with your children. Visit your grandparents, take time for your health, and periodically get a medical checkup. Be sure to take your spouse out to a nice dinner. Go out and hit the greens and play another eighteen holes. There will always be time to clean the house and fix the disposal, so take care of the golf balls first because they are the things that really matter in life. Be sure to set your priorities because the rest is just sand."

At that point, one of the students raised her hand and inquired about what the beer represents. The old professor just smiled and said, "I'm glad that you asked. The beer simply shows you that no matter how full your life may seem, there is always room for a couple of beers with a friend."

These are life lessons that we all can identify with. Let's not let our lives get so full of the day-to-day living that we forget to live, that we don't take the time to listen to our children, that we fail to give them the nurturing and attention that they need for their development. Sometimes we are so busy flying from place to place to make ends meet that we become disconnected with those closest to us. When we break the circuit, the light goes out. Reconnect that same circuit, the light returns. As it is with our lives, the relationships that we develop are our circuits, and the broken relationships that we develop are the circuit breakers. As long as there is a complete circuit, we are in the light. As soon as the breaker is tripped, we are immediately thrust into darkness. At this point, we depend completely on our touching a nearby object to study our position.

Education and Christianity are our way to the light switch and our way out of darkness. *The Journal of Blacks in Higher Education* states that nationally, the black student college graduation rate remains a dismally low 43 percent. But the college completion rate has improved by four percentage points over the past three years (2005–2009). As ever, the black-white gap in college graduation rates remains very large, and little to no progress has been achieved in bridging the divide. William J. Edwards, Assistant Professor of Biology at Niagara University, stated that "education is the source of all we have and the springboard for all our future joys."

Christianity has played a major role in my life. I was forever in church for choir rehearsals, Bible study, prayer meetings, etc. These initiatives were a tremendous help in establishing self-esteem, character, confidence, and belief in God. Religion has been the backbone for many of us, no matter the race or culture. It gives us a true beginning and it helps us determine what is considered right from wrong. It tends to cause us to take the right fork in the road, do the right thing, have a clear conscience, keep our family together, and it adds stability to our daily lives. Now that's how we see it affecting us. How does it affect you? We face a society that can be cajoling and menacing, and religion, Christianity, and fellowship have a calming effect on these worldly conditions.

ABOUT THE AUTHOR

Ted Bagley, vice president of human resources at Amgen Pharmaceutical Company in Thousand Oaks, California, was born in Birmingham, Alabama, to Ted and Eddie Mae Bagley, both deceased. His brother, William Bagley, recently retired, resides in Indianapolis with his wife, Larnell, and daughter, Jennifer.

After graduating from high school, Ted joined Uncle Sam's Army, where he served in the Old Guard, a ceremonial unit in Fort Myer, Virginia. After serving for several years in that prestigious unit, he was sent to Vietnam at the height of the conflict. At the end of his military career, Ted continued his education at Ohio State University and later graduated from Franklin Business Law School in Columbus, Ohio. After college, he joined the General Electric Company's world-renowned executive leadership program. After working his way to the executive ranks, Ted left GE to join the Russell Corporation based in Atlanta, Georgia. After several years with Russell, he joined Dell Computer in Nashville, Tennessee.

His hobbies are bike riding, reading, writing, skating, and minor car repair. He has a wife, Debra, current chair for the Ventura County Women's Commission, and four children, Marcus, Chantal, Christopher, and Jared. His passions are public speaking, counseling, working with young people, and exercising. He currently has another piece of his work in publication. The book's title is *My Personal War Within*. It's scheduled to be released in April 2011.